Confessions of a
Teen Sleuth

By the same author

The Hippie Handbook: How to Tie-Dye a T-Shirt, Flash a Peace Sign,
and Other Essential Skills for the Carefree Life
Dharma Girl: A Road Trip Across the American Generations

As editor

Wild Child: Girlhoods in the Counterculture

Confessions of a Teen Sleuth

A Parody by

Chelsea Cain

Illustrations by Lia Miternique

BLOOMSBURY

Published by Bloomsbury Publishing, New York and London
Distributed to the trade by Holtzbrinck Publishers

All papers used by Bloomsbury Publishing are natural, recyclable
products made from wood grown in well-managed forests.
The manufacturing processes conform to the environmental
regulations of the country of origin.

Library of Congress Cataloging-in-Publication Data

Cain, Chelsea.
Confessions of a teen sleuth :
a parody / by Chelsea Cain
illustrations by Lia Miternique.—1st U.S. ed.
p. cm.
ISBN 1–58234–511–2
1. American wit and humor. 2. Keene, Carolyn—Parodies, imitations, etc.
3. Drew, Nancy (Fictitious character)—Humor. I. Title.

PN6231.P3C25 2004
813'.6—dc22
2004013972

ISBN-13 9781582345116

First U.S. Edition 2005

1 3 5 7 9 10 8 6 4 2

Typeset by Hewer Text Ltd, Edinburgh
Printed in the United States of America
by Quebecor World Fairfield

CONTENTS

For Frank Hardy

Nunc scio quit sit amor.

—Virgil

INTRODUCTION

If you are reading this, then I am gone and this manuscript, per my instruction, has been delivered to the writer Chelsea Cain for publication as she sees fit. I chose Ms. Cain as my editor based on the merits of her four-volume Trixie Belden biography, which won the National Book Award last year.

As many of you know me only as a character in a series of books written by a former friend of mine named Carolyn Keene, let me make one thing clear: Carolyn Keene used my name without my permission and made a career for herself telling stories of my adventures, many of which were fraught with error and some of which were patently false.

Why did I wait all these years to come forward? Of course I wrote Carolyn's publisher, but they insisted that I was a fictional character developed by a think tank and written by a confederate of writers led by Edward Stratemeyer and that Carolyn Keene didn't exist! Defeated, I watched as Carolyn made a name for herself pillaging my life's work.

I feared that if I revealed myself, details might come to light that could embarrass my husband and child. I have lived with that fear too long and have come to understand that the truth must be known regardless of its consequences. And so it is only now, in the twilight of my life, that I feel that it is time to set the record straight.

Nancy Drew
River Heights, Illinois
1992

I THE HIDDEN HARDY, 1926

Readers of Carolyn Keene's version of my life's events may be surprised to learn that Ned Nickerson was not the love of my life. In fact, my heart belonged to another. I first met Frank Hardy in the summer of 1925. He and his younger brother, Joe, had come to town from Bayport, New Jersey, on the trail of a missing waitress. I was walking out of Jackson's Drug Store when I saw them pull up on their red Indian Scout motorcycles. Even soiled from their five-day journey, they were both striking. Frank was wearing khaki pants, a collared shirt, and a maroon sweater. Joe was wearing the same clothes, only his sweater was blue. They even had the same haircut, though Frank's hair was darker. Yet to me they could not have been more different. I could tell immediately that Frank was the older, more experienced of the two brothers. He held himself taller and walked with the subtle swagger of a boy older than his seventeen years. I approached them—they had parked their Scouts in a no-parking zone—and soon found myself swept up in their mystery. We found their missing waitress working the morning shift at Oscar Peterson's Bakery, and the two soon returned to Bayport. I never thought I'd see Frank again. Until that next summer when the doorbell rang.

I had just solved the Mystery at Lilac Inn and was unpacking my tasteful blue luggage when I heard our housekeeper,

Hannah Gruen, answer the door. Hannah was only in her midthirties then, though a youth spent smoking unfiltered Luckys had aged her prematurely. She wore her fair hair in a bun and her skirts long, though I had seen her more than once leave the house in trousers when my father was away on business. Curious as to the identity of our visitor, I craned to look around the upstairs corner and saw the back of Frank's head as Hannah took his coat. My heart leapt in my chest.

I smoothed my stylish coif, adjusted my loose knit jacket, and went downstairs.

"Frank," I announced maturely. "How good to see you again."

I extended my hand, and Frank took it, grinning.

"Nancy," he responded. "It's a pleasure. It's good to see you looking as slim and attractive as always." Then his face grew grave. "But enough pleasantries. I'm here because something has happened to Joe and I need your help."

I nodded solemnly, but even as I did my heart swelled. He needed my help. Of all the teen sleuths he knew (and rumor was he knew plenty), he had come to me.

Before we could say another word, the doorbell rang again. Hannah answered it. She turned to me, her cheeks flushed with excitement. "Nancy!" she gasped. "It's a letter for you. Special delivery!"

Hannah Gruen and Frank Hardy gathered around me as I opened the mysterious letter that had just arrived.

"Who's it from?" asked the housekeeper.

"I don't know," I answered. "There's no return address." I opened the letter carefully so as not to destroy any clues. Inside was a typewritten note:

"STAY OUT OF IT," the note warned.

I looked up at Frank, who stood gazing intently at the letter. "Maybe you had better tell me a little more about what happened to Joe," I told him.

Hannah went to the kitchen to make tea while Frank and I sat in the living room, the typed note on the coffee table between us.

"Joe has been penning mash notes to Helen Corning for months. She finally agreed to meet him if he came to River Heights," Frank explained glumly. (Helen was three years older than I so had already graduated from R.H. High and was in heady pursuit of a husband.) "But she had to cancel at the last minute," Frank continued. "I called Jake's Ice Cream Parlor where they were supposed to rendezvous, and Jake said that Joe waited for an hour and then left. This was two days ago, and he has yet to surface!"

I folded my hands neatly in my lap. "Is he a drinker?"

Frank shifted uncomfortably in his seat. "He likes to bend an elbow from time to time."

We locked eyes. I could feel a warm rush of passion swell in my bosom. "We'll find him," I told Frank breathlessly. "We'll find your brother Joe." I stood up and reached for my expensive camel hair coat, cloche hat, and aviator goggles. "Come on," I exclaimed, looking back at Frank. "There's only one place to get an illicit drink in this town: The Green Jade Café. We haven't a moment to lose!"

Frank and I sped along the country road in my custom blue Ford Roadster. We had just passed Riverside Park and the Bridle Path when I heard a piercing scream.

I froze behind the wheel. Had I inadvertently hit someone

again? The judge had let me off the first time, but a second would be manslaughter for sure! My heart pounded in fright as I opened the car door to step out.

At that instant a shadowy figure arose from a pile of hay nearby. The attractive young man was wearing a full-length raccoon coat, popular in those days with the college set. "Hi, Nancy," the young man greeted me bashfully.

I removed my goggles. "Ned?"

"You know this fellow?" asked Frank.

"Yes," I pouted. "Ned, what are you doing here? Are you following me again?"

Ned looked at his shoes. "I was just worried about you," he muttered. "I phoned and Mrs. Gruen told me what was going on. I figured you were headed to the Green Jade Café so I thought I'd beat you there. But then my scooter ran out of gas. I was hiding in the hay pile when a chicken startled me. That's when you drove up."

"Who is this cat?" Frank asked me.

Ned stood up a little. "I'm her special friend," he explained. "Omega Chi Epsilon."

Frank looked at me questioningly. I shrugged.

A few minutes later Ned had strapped his scooter to my trunk and the three of us were racing toward our destination.

The Green Jade Café was in Dockville, a slum area near the Muskoka, the river that divides my hometown. A tributary of the Mississippi, the Muskoka of my youth was still crystal clear and I cruised it often as a member of the River Heights Yacht Club. Of course these days most people know the

"You know this fellow?" asked Frank.

Muskoka as one of the first EPA Superfund cleanup sites in the 1980s.

The pavement in Dockville was poor, and there were rows upon rows of tenement houses punctuated by fortune-tellers and thrift shops. The residents were mostly domestic workers, recent immigrants, petty criminals, and others down on their luck. This was an area rarely mentioned in the River Heights *Morning Record*. (Unlike my own exploits, which were often front-page news. With photos.)

We arrived at the Green Jade Café only to find it closed. As it was early evening on a weekday, using my detective prowess, I deduced that this was suspicious.

"I guess we should just go home," suggested Ned.

But peering through the glass front door, I thought I caught the sight of movement. I tried the door. It opened.

"Nancy!" Ned gasped.

I took a step inside. Frank followed. Ned followed behind Frank.

The Green Jade Café was a speakeasy that specialized in plying patrons with fraudulent palm readings once they had imbibed several ounces of malt whiskey. Everyone knew it existed, including Chief McGinnis, but it was allowed to operate due to the protection of several members of the city council.

Inside, the walls were painted emerald green, and a dark wooden bar loomed huge on one wall. Several chairs were scattered on the floor.

"There's been a fight!" reported Frank.

"Shh!" I ordered. "Listen!"

From deep inside the café came a distant moan.

"Jiminy crickets!" exclaimed Ned.

The three of us moved through the café toward the faint groaning noise coming from what seemed to be the kitchen area.

"There!" Frank cried, pointing to a closet at the back of the room. "The noise seems to be coming from behind that door!"

Putting my finger over my lips, I reached toward the doorknob and turned it. It was locked. I took off my hat, pulled a bobby pin from my smart hairdo and, kneeling in my slimming skirt, quickly and expertly picked the closet lock. Then I stood, took a step back, and opened the door.

A fair-haired young man was curled at the bottom of the closet, his arms and legs bound and a handkerchief tied across his mouth.

"Joe!" wept Frank. He quickly cut the cords that bound his brother and lifted him out of the closet, trembling, into his arms.

My momentary fright gone, I let my guard down. It was a split second later that I felt the blanket come down over my head and wrap tightly around me.

I screamed and struggled as my assailant attempted to drag me backward toward an uncertain fate. I could hear a scuffle and assumed that the boys were facing similar assaults.

My arms were pinned underneath the blanket, and I could feel my attacker's arms wrapped snuggly around my waist, holding the blanket and my own arms in place. Unable to free myself, I bent my knees and flailed my legs in hopes of making contact. I screamed again and a hand wrapped tightly over my mouth. Suddenly my senses were overcome with a strong odor. Chloroform, I thought. Then I blacked out.

I awoke in a small dimly lit room that I identified immediately as a pantry of some sort. I instantly deduced that I was most likely still in the Green Jade Café. My head throbbed, my tongue felt heavy, and my titian hair was mussed, but I was not restrained. I sat up.

"Nancy, are you okay?" asked a voice in the corner.

It was Frank.

"I think so," I answered steadily. "Where are the others?"

"I don't know," he sighed glumly. "I woke up in here."

I got up and tried the door. It was locked. I fumbled for a bobby pin. They were all gone! My hair was completely undone!

I slunk over to Frank and sat down beside him.

"So who's this Ned person?" he asked.

"Oh, we've dated forever," I sighed. "He goes to Emerson. I'm always having to get him out of jams. You know, kidnapping, quicksand, wild dogs. But he's dark haired and handsome, and he's captain of the football team."

"But do you love him?"

"I love rescuing him when he's been taken prisoner."

Frank was very near me now, and I could feel my heart race at his proximity. I cleared my throat.

"And you? Do you have a girlfriend?" I asked.

He smiled. "No one serious," he answered with a twinkle in his eye.

The he reached his hand behind my head, firmly pulled me toward him, and kissed me.

It was a full hour later when I noticed the ventilator duct above our heads.

"Frank!" I exclaimed, adjusting my blouse. "Look at that! Lift me up, and I bet I'll be able to climb out and open the door."

Frank lifted me by my hips, and I was able to reach up to the vent, remove the grate, and pull myself into the small square duct. I shimmied several feet and found myself at another vent that exited into the kitchen of the Green Jade Café. After ascertaining that the coast was clear, I carefully lowered myself to the floor and, retracing my route through the duct, found the pantry where Frank and I had been held captive. The key was in the lock! Within moments, Frank was free and we set out to find the others.

We found them tied to chairs in a back room behind the kitchen. They were dressed in striped shirts and wool pants, the sailor outfits of the day. Their captors, two mustachioed gentlemen with tattooed forearms and large gold hoop earrings in one ear, hovered over them, scowling. "Gypsy pirates," I mouthed to Frank.

Joe and Ned were being shanghaied!

Without thought to my own personal safety, I rushed in and karate-chopped one of the pirates firmly across the back of the neck. He fell to the ground with a thud. Frank, a few steps behind me, socked the other pirate across the jaw. The pirate stumbled for a moment and then also fell to the floor, unconscious.

Frank and I quickly untied the boys.

"Oh, Ned!" I cried, throwing my arms around him.

"They were going to sell us to a riverboat captain," cried Joe. "He was going to take us to New Orleans and then send us on a ship to the Orient! I came here to get a drink after Helen Corning stood me up, and the next thing I knew I was in that closet where you found me!"

"Helen didn't stand you up," explained Frank gently. "Her great-aunt Rosemary was taken ill. She called, but you didn't get the message."

Joe looked chagrined.

Ned gaped at me gratefully, his eyes wet. "You saved me," he cried.

One of the pirates stirred on the floor.

"I'd better call Chief McGinnis," I exclaimed, heading toward the phone behind the bar.

Ten minutes later the chief and several of River Heights's finest were milling around the café, and the pirates were in custody.

"Nancy, you're a hero," declared Chief McGinnis. "You broke up a massive shanghai operation."

"I had plenty of help," I replied, glancing over at Frank. "I'm just happy that we could make a difference."

"What about the note?" Ned asked.

"The pirates must have found out that Frank was coming to town to look for Joe. They sent the note to my house to try to intimidate us," I explained.

"Fat chance," Ned declared adoringly.

I walked over to where Frank was standing. "I guess we did it," I told him.

His brown eyes bored deeply into mine, and I felt my pulse quicken. "Bayport is a bit of a hoof, but I have to say I like the cut of your jib."

I glanced over at Ned talking to the chief. "Ned needs me," I explained. Then I hugged Frank. "We'll meet again," I whispered into his ear.

And we did.

II THE REAL SECRET
OF THE OLD CLOCK, 1929

Carolyn Keene stomped her foot petulantly. "Nancy Drew!" she exclaimed. "We're never going to be ready at this rate!"

The plump, dark-haired girl had been my roommate at Bryn Mawr for nearly two months. I had taken Carolyn, a somewhat dull creature, under my wing, introducing her to my chums and including her in some of the many events for which I served as chair. Now she looked very cunning in my hand-beaded, powder pink, chiffon shift, and was clearly delighted to be attending the school-sponsored "Foxtrot for Lady Factory Workers" as a date of my special friend Ned's chum Dave Evans.

I had been worried about Carolyn. She had come to college on scholarship from Iowa, where she had been raised on a hog farm. She didn't speak of her parents much, but I knew she missed the animals terribly. She wanted to be some sort of writer but was flunking all her writing courses and showed little promise of improvement. Now her cheeks were flushed and her eyes danced with excitement at the thought of our double date.

I finished slipping into my smart tweed skirt and silk blouse, and ran a comb through my titian hair. I had just checked my reflection—slim and attractive, as always—when there was a knock on our dorm room door.

Ned Nickerson, captain of the Emerson College football team, and Dave Evans, tight end, stood in the doorway, grinning. Dave had dated my chum George, a tomboyish girl who had broken up with him shortly after beginning school at Smith College.

"Leaping catfish!" gushed Ned, looking mostly at me. "You two look aces!"

Carolyn blushed deeply.

We had just put on our coats and were about to exit when a tall, distinguished gentleman appeared behind the boys. It was Professor Dartman, a freshman historical lit teacher at the college.

"I'm sorry to interrupt your fun, Nancy," he apologized, "but something terrible has happened!"

A short time later we were all gathered in Professor Dartman's spacious wood-paneled office. He gravely explained that he had come back to his office for some papers and discovered that a window had been broken and the office had been ransacked! He recalled that I had written my college admissions essay on "Teen Sleuthing and the Aesthetics of Ambivalence" and immediately came to find me.

I was pleasantly gratified that my reputation as an amateur detective had preceded me. "Is anything missing?" I inquired.

"Yes! A clock that belonged to my grandfather."

"A clock?" retorted Carolyn, placing her little fists on her generous hips. "You're making us late to the benefit hop because of a stupid clock?"

I shot Carolyn a quieting look and she sank into a chair.

"Do you have any enemies?" I continued.

16

Professor Dartman shook his head. "None that I know of."

I extracted my magnifying glass from my pretty beaded evening bag and instructed the gang to stand back while I searched for clues. And hour later I had finished scouring the desk and had moved on to the carpet, when Carolyn stood up in disgust.

"I don't know why he doesn't just call the police!" she exclaimed. "I'm going to the dance with or without the rest of you."

She took a step and screamed.

Carolyn lifted up her Mary Jane in despair. She had stepped right into a pool of foul-smelling liquid.

"Don't move," I instructed. I went over and examined the liquid under my magnifying glass. "Professor Dartman," I asked carefully, "do you know any bootleggers?"

Professor Dartman paled. But before he could speak, the room was thrown into darkness!

I felt someone rush past me, and then the lights were flung back on. My heart was racing. I looked around the room. Ned stood at the light switch by the door, his eyes bright with excitement. Dave still sat in his chair. Professor Dartman sat at his desk, wide-eyed and stammering. But Carolyn was missing!

The French doors facing the student quad were wide open.

"I'll go for help!" cried Dave, standing up and running from the room.

I surveyed the quad. There was no sign of any telltale footprints or snapped twigs, and certainly no sign of Carolyn or her kidnapper.

"The thief must have been hiding in the closet!" exclaimed Ned, pointing in dismay to the open closet door.

"Professor Dartman," I asked carefully,
"do you know any bootleggers?"

"I agree," I agreed. "This is now a matter for the police. I will call my good friend Chief McGinnis personally." Though he worked in River Heights, I happened to know that Chief McGinnis was in Philadelphia attending an Athletics/Cubs World Series game. I called the chief at his hotel, and after I explained the situation, he agreed to come to campus as soon as possible to investigate.

I relayed this information to Ned and Professor Dartman. "Before the chief gets here," I asked Professor Dartman, "do you want to tell me how a man of your stature became involved in a bootlegging ring?"

Professor Dartman's face fell. "How did you know?" he quavered.

"It was as clear as the nose on your face," I retorted. "One guess is as good as another, but I'd say that your interest in mysticism drew you to it." I gestured around the office to the Haitian voodoo sculptures and Pyrenean memory masks that adorned the walls. "Everyone knows that Hank Cutthroat, the infamous Chicago bootlegger, is a scholar of Celtic mysticism. What did he promise you for your cooperation, Professor? The secret to Stonehenge?"

Professor Dartman began to cry, nodding his head in affirmation. "He swore to me that he would give me the power of the Celtic priests if I would only sell hooch to fraternity boys. It seemed a small price to pay."

"That hooch comes from you?" asked Ned.

"But what would Hank Cutthroat and his henchmen want with an old clock? Or with Carolyn?" I mused. "Unless . . . Carolyn is the thief!"

★ ★ ★

19

When Chief McGinnis arrived, he took Professor Dartman into custody for hooch pedding, and I relayed my suspicions to him about Carolyn and the old clock. Dave had returned to Emerson, having found Carolyn too plump for his taste anyway.

After our interview with Chief McGinnis, Ned escorted me back to my dorm.

"You know," he teased, slipping his arm in mine, "I'll be graduating in a few months. I was thinking it might be a good time to make plans."

"Plans?"

"You said we could get engaged after college. I've been putting all my extra money in the stock market." He smiled engagingly. "It can't go anywhere but up."

I gazed at Ned's handsome, blank features. "I've been taking these classes about patriarchy in society and they've got me thinking . . ."

Ned set his jaw and nodded. "I can wait," he declared bravely. "In the meantime, I've got to find a new source for hooch."

I watched him go off alone, then turned and headed for my dorm. I had just entered my empty room when I felt the cold edge of steel at my throat.

Before I could react, someone forced me roughly to my desk chair, where I was tied tightly to the chair from behind!

"You think you're so smart, Nancy Drew," sobbed a voice behind me.

I would have known that voice anywhere. It was my roommate, Carolyn Keene!

Carolyn stood in front of me. She had changed out of my hand-beaded, powder pink, chiffon shift and had squeezed into one of my slimming skirts and blouses. The skirt was drawn taut against her stout thighs and was partially unzipped. The blouse was small in the shoulders, and the pearl buttons threatened to burst over her ample bosom.

"How do you think it makes me feel," cried Carolyn, pressing the knife against my throat, "to hear you go on and on and on about your adventures? You're always talking about the Hidden Staircase, the Clue in the Jewel Box, the Crooked Bannister, blah blah blah. Oh, you're so perfect. So popular. With your perfect boyfriend and your skirts." Tears were streaming down Carolyn's plump cheeks. "I just wanted to be part of the adventure. Just once. I wanted Professor Dartman to come to me to help him find his old clock. He knows I love old clocks. Old clocks and hogs. When he came to you, I decided to fake my kidnapping. So you would rescue me. But you didn't even look."

"We looked," I lied. "We just couldn't find you."

"Couldn't find me? The great Nancy Drew? Teen sleuth?"

"That's right, Carolyn. You outsmarted me."

"I outsmarted you?"

"Uh-huh. Now put down the knife."

Carolyn sniffed and wiped away a tear. "I just wanted to be part of your story," she faltered, letting the knife drop to the floor. Then she knelt behind me, struggling in the tight skirt, still weeping, and untied the ropes before melting into a heap of tears.

"So what's going to happen to her?" asked Ned. It was a week after the incident and we were sitting on a bench in the quad sharing a malted.

"I decided not to press charges," I explained. "But the college sent her home to the hog farm. It turns out she has an addiction to Uncle Ezra Pinex Cough Syrup. They found dozens of empty bottles hidden under her bed. They think it may have contributed to her nervous breakdown."

"Do you think she'll be all right?"

"I don't know. I hope so. The strange thing is that they found all these papers under her bed too. Like diaries. Only they were all about me. She had taken notes on all the stories I ever told her about back home. About you and Bess and George and everyone." I shivered. "She got a lot of stuff wrong, but it was still unnerving."

"What do you think she's going to do with all that stuff?" asked Ned.

"Who knows? But they sent it to her at the hog farm with all her other belongings."

Ned took my hand and held it. "I'm just glad it's over," he sighed. "And at least there's a bright side."

"What's that?" I asked.

"You'll never have to hear the name Carolyn Keene again."

III THE CLUE IN THE
NAZI NUTCRACKER, 1942

"I want to kill Nazis more than anything!" declared Ned. I patted his hand. We were sitting at the small kitchen table in our Chicago walk-up, located in a brick apartment building on a wide, tree-lined street. We had moved there shortly after our marriage.

"I've heard some pretty frightening things about Nazis," I commented. "Besides, it's not your fault that you hurt your knee in that big Emerson football game."

"But Burt and Dave got to go!" Ned cried.

"They passed their physicals," I sighed. I stood up from the table and smoothed my fitted skirt over my still-attractive figure. "Shouldn't you be getting to the slaughterhouse?" I asked, admiring the reflection of my rolled, shoulder-length titian hair in the chrome handle of the Frigidaire.

Ned nodded and stood. He was still tall, with an athletic build and brown hair and eyes, but his eyes twinkled less, and the things that used to fascinate him, like secret passageways, flying, and voodoo, seemed to hold little interest. It might have had something to do with the job he took as a meat inspector. All day long he toured the city's slaughterhouses, ensuring that the cattle were slaughtered in the least egregious manner and that the number of mice and rats ground into the all-beef chub was minimal. It was his contribution to the war effort. Ned longed to have a son to whom he could teach the finer points of agricultural codes and football. I was thirty-two at this point, and if we were to have children it would have to be soon, but I still clung to my independence, despite social and personal pressures. It was a source of tension in our otherwise tranquil relationship.

Ned had just left and I was clearing the dishes (how I missed plump and motherly Hannah Gruen!) when I heard light footsteps from below. Someone was coming up the staircase! I stood frozen as my complexion paled. Remaining courageous and levelheaded, I forced myself to tilt my head slightly toward the door and listen.

"Nancy?" called a woman's anxious voice.

I fairly flew to the front door and flung it open.

"Bess!" I cried, throwing my arms around the cleverly dressed woman standing at the threshold. "I had a hunch it was you!"

Bess Marvin, my old childhood chum and detecting pal, hugged me tightly. She was still blond haired, blue eyed, and pretty. Though Carolyn Keene cruelly described Bess as "overweight," Bess never had a weight problem and was in fact quite slender. It was Carolyn who was the chubby one. I had introduced the two at a Bryn Mawr house party, and Carolyn felt slighted when several Penn men had surrounded Bess and ignored Carolyn. Clearly the slanderous references to my friend's plumpness were nothing more than a petty attempt at revenge on Carolyn's part. As the books became more popular, Bess was nearly destroyed by the constant mockery of her girth and grew quite anorexic in the 1930s. She had been married and divorced twice. Now standing before me, Bess was still underweight, but she looked far healthier than six months before when her cousin George and I had put her on the train to McLean Hospital, a sanitarium near Boston. Back then shoulder pads alone could add five pounds.

"Welcome home!" I exclaimed.

"Oh, Nancy, haven't you heard?" Bess's blue eyes filled with tears.

"What?" I asked fretfully.

Her painted bottom lip trembled. "It's Joe Hardy! He's been killed in the war!"

That night I packed a suitcase of cap-sleeved blouses, fitted suits, and other essentials, and the next morning we were on a train to Bayport. It was just us two girls. Ned was needed at the sausage plant. George, Bess's tomboyish cousin and my other best childhood chum, was working as a riveter in the River Heights industrial district and had arranged to meet us in New Jersey. Bess dabbed at her cheeks with a hankie. She had always felt a fondness for Joe. The two had dated briefly and, upon parting, he had presented her with a copy of *The Scarlet Letter*, which she had enjoyed thoroughly despite having only skimmed it. She credited this early creative exercise with defining her chosen career path: condensing novels for *Reader's Digest*. She made a good living at it and could work from home on her Underwood Universal portable typewriter.

Outside the landscape flew by, a picturesque horizon of meadows, rivers, waterwheels, and small towns.

I should clarify now a subject of much controversy: the geographical location of my hometown. Some readers of Carolyn's books believe it to be in the Midwest, some believe it to be on the East Coast (Carolyn was always sloppy with geography). Let me set the record straight once and for all: River Heights is located in central Illinois, twenty miles west of Peoria. If anyone had ever bothered to check a map this would have been abundantly clear.

I was only half paying attention to the blur out the train window. My head was spinning. I still couldn't believe that Joe was gone. Of course I would know plenty of boys who would die in the war. Friends. Neighbors. Other sleuths. But Joe was the first one to die whom I had once rescued. My heart ached for Frank. He and his little brother were inseparable through-out their late teens, and Frank had always relished his role as Joe's protector and chief dating rival. I worried that Joe's death would leave Frank reeling for years to come.

I relayed my thoughts to Bess.

"I'm sure he'll be devastated," Bess agreed.

I explained that Frank and I had lost touch after he refused to attend Ned's and my wedding and instead gone on a scenic aerial tour of the Grand Canyon with that tart Helen Corning. Bess told me that I had already told her that story.

"I guess I'm just nervous," I shrugged.

We arrived in Bayport late the next morning. George, who had arrived earlier that day on the River Heights express, picked us up at the train station. Always an athletic girl who enjoyed her boy's name, George had bulked up even more due to her hours of riveting fighter plane fuselages. She still wore her brown hair short, preferred wide-legged trousers to skirts, and had taken to wearing sleeveless blouses to show off her brawny biceps.

"Hypers!" she exclaimed when she saw us. "You two look beat!"

On the way to the Hardy house at the corner of High and Elm, George explained that Joe's plane had been shot down over Germany. There were no survivors. Frank had been in Washington, where he worked for a top secret intelligence-gathering organization, and was expected back that evening. Fenton Hardy, the boys' father, had once been a crack detective on the New York City police force before retiring to Bayport many years before to work as a private investigator. Rumor had it he was now consulting with the navy, using a flashlight on their rooftop at night to signal to submarines in Barmet Bay.

The boys' aunt Gertrude met us at the door to the large, comfortably furnished Hardy home. Tall and angular, Aunt Gertrude still cut an imposing figure despite her advanced years. Decades of cookie baking had left her with especially large thighs.

"I'm so sorry," I stammered on behalf of our group.

"I told him that joining the air force was a bad idea," Aunt Gertrude snorted sadly. She led us into the fashionable living room, where Fenton Hardy and his trim, pretty, middle-aged wife, Laura, sat on the floral print sofa. Mrs. Hardy wept softly on Mr. Hardy's sweater. I had never met Frank and Joe's mother before and had assumed that she was dead. Faced with clear evidence to the contrary, I now found myself in an awkward spot! But I quickly recovered my composure and stepped forward to offer my condolences.

Bess, George, and I had unpacked and settled into the upstairs guest room, and I was waiting to use the only bathroom in the Hardy home, when Frank appeared at the top of the stairs. He

27

was wearing his army uniform and carrying a khaki duffel bag and a briefcase full of secret dossiers. He had grown even more handsome, his face creased with maturity. He saw me and stopped in his tracks, and I found myself suddenly self-conscious of my sheer baby blue mini-nightie and mules.

"Hello, Frank," I gushed.

"Nancy!" he grinned, looking me up and down. "Seeing you always makes me tingle."

I swallowed hard and clutched the sheer fabric that was the only barrier between my bosom and his chest of medals. "I was so sorry to hear about Joe," I managed.

He took another step toward me. "Yes," he murmured. "I will miss him very much. We shared a room for eighteen years. It will be strange to sleep alone in this big house tonight."

My breath ached in my chest. I tried to speak, but my mouth was too dry.

"So," Frank continued, "I'll see you in the morning at the funeral?" He took a step back, and I regained my speech with a sputter.

"Yes. Tomorrow. The funeral."

He nodded, then turned and continued down the hall toward the room he had shared with his brother.

The bathroom door opened and Bess popped her head out. Her hair was wrapped in a large towel, and she was wearing yellow pajamas. "What was that?" she asked. "I thought I heard you talking to someone."

I sighed and felt my knees shudder. "Frank's home," I answered.

★   ★   ★

I tried to speak, but my mouth was too dry.

Several other sleuths attended the funeral to pay their respects: Cherry Ames, who was still a student nurse at Spencer Hospital School of Nursing but hoped to join the Army Nurse Corps, was present, as was Vicki Barr, a stewardess with Federal Airlines, who had once dated Joe. Louise and Jean Dana, who had stopped speaking to one another for a year after a difficult, Joe-centered love triangle, made the drive from Oak Falls. Many of the men were away working for the war effort. Tom Swift Senior sent a nice card postmarked Los Alamos. Aviator Ted Scott sent a telegram from the South Pacific. Several notable friends were missing. Frank and Joe's best chum, Chet Morton, was a grunt on the front lines, and Bert and Freddie Bobbsey had died in the Pacific just months apart from one another the year before. Flossie Bobbsey, now a professional birth control advocate, kindly drove down from New York.

The Bayport set also was present. Callie Shaw, Frank's vivacious, petite ex-girlfriend, and Iola Morton, Joe's wife and Chet's sister, bravely clung to one another through their tears. Chief Ezra Collig, Dr. Bates, and Jerry Gilroy were all pallbearers.

The service was brief and heartfelt. The Dana girls sobbed uncontrollably. We lowered Joe's casket into the ground, and the air force officers presented Mrs. Hardy with the flag from his coffin. Afterward, we all retreated to the Hardy home for a postfuneral gathering and some of Aunt Gertrude's fresh-baked cookies.

"I can't believe how much Cherry is flirting with Frank," I whispered to Bess and George.

Bess rolled her eyes in agreement and headed for the punch bowl.

As the evening passed, Cherry remained glued to Frank's side. I could tell that Frank was trying desperately to get away, but Cherry was making it impossible! I was becoming extremely worried. Did Cherry plan to take advantage of Frank's vulnerable state? There was no time to speculate.

I hurried up to Frank, glancing at my wristwatch, "Goodness!" I exclaimed. "Frank, if we don't leave at once, we'll miss the séance!"

Cherry tossed her head, sending her dark brown curls cascading off her glowing cheeks. "Honestly, Nancy," she exclaimed, "if you weren't a friend of Frank's, I'd cut you up for stew and feed you to my worst enemy."

"Nice uniform," I retorted, glancing down at her crackling white nurse's apron.

"At least I change uniforms sometimes," Cherry countered. "You're wearing the same exact skirt you had on when we met." She looked me up and down. "And it's looking a little tight around the hips."

"Girls," Frank intervened. He put his hand on the small of my back and led me away to the back porch, leaving Cherry glaring behind us.

"What's got into you?" he asked. His breath felt hot on my face.

"I'm just so bent out of shape about Joe!" I stammered. "It's such a tragedy!"

Frank's eyes twinkled. "Nancy, you're as hard to read as a Turkish mannequin."

I smiled, but my head was spinning. Joe was dead. You live your whole life thinking you're doing the right thing. You marry your special friend. You move to Chicago. Then something happens and everything goes catawampus. "Jeepers, Frank," I gushed before I could stop myself, "I think I'm in love with you!"

"What about Nick?"

"Ned."

"Ned."

"I love him too, I guess. He's just so . . . boring."

Frank took me by my shoulders. There was a challenge in his eye. "Nancy," he asked, "do you trust me?"

I shuddered. "With everything I have," I answered.

"Then I'm going to ask you to trust me right now."

Before I could retort, a great silver orb appeared over Frank's left shoulder. Though I had never seen one, I knew it immediately. A dirigible! And it was landing in the Hardys' backyard!

"We have to leave immediately," Frank ordered. "No time for good-byes. Joe is alive. And he's being held captive in Germany. We may be the only two people who can get him out of this pickle. Are you up for it?"

Joe? Still alive? Germany? Joe needed me. My country needed me. I stared him squarely in the eye and nodded. "I'm ready."

The dirigible took us to a top secret airfield in Queens. I phoned Ned and told him that I was spending a few extra days with Cherry Ames and Vicki Barr in Atlantic City. Then we boarded a military airplane and flew across the Atlantic. On the trip, Frank explained the predicament.

Joe had been sent on an urgent mission. He was on the trail of a nutcracker that had been forged by a Russian jeweler. It

32

had ended up the property of a fat rich man in Zurich, then was sold to a French movie star, who lost it in a divorce to a Dominican playboy, who sold it to an anonymous collector, who donated it to the British Museum in London. Then, two months ago, it had been stolen! Scotland Yard had turned up only one clue at the scene: a tiny brooch in the form of a swastika!

"But what would the Nazis want with a nutcracker?" I asked incredulously.

"That's exactly what we wanted to know," answered Frank. "So we sent Joe behind enemy lines to find out. Last we heard from him, he had a meeting with an Austrian countess he said might have the answer. That was last week. No one has heard from him since."

"But you think he's still alive?"

"Absolutely. Joe gets into jams, but he never dies. Of course, we can't let the enemy know that we know that he's been captured."

"So you had the funeral."

"Exactly." For a moment Frank looked uncharacteristically grim. "This is a dangerous mission. And I needed the best in the business. I've always thought highly of your sleuthing abilities, and when I remembered that you took high school German, well, I just knew that you were the one." He set his jaw in determination. "The fate of the free world may just rest with this nutcracker." Frank glanced out the window into the black night over the Atlantic. "You can skydive, right?"

We stripped off our parachutes and hid them in a barn on a farm just outside of Berlin. We had parachuted just before sunrise and then settled down to catch a few hours of sleep in the hayloft. Neither of us got much rest.

I awoke first and made Frank a breakfast of fresh eggs on our government issued hot plate. After we had eaten, we changed into our disguises. Frank wore a Nazi uniform, while I braided my hair and wore the attire of a common German girl. We liberated two bicycles that were in the barn and rode them casually into town, admiring the rural landscape and whistling a German drinking song so as not to arouse suspicion.

Frank had the countess's address, so we pedaled there first. It was a tall stone town house surrounded by a large wrought-iron fence.

"Look!" I whispered. A red banner emblazoned with a swastika flew from one of the house's high windows. The countess was a Nazi!

Frank nodded grimly and headed through the gate for the front door.

A diminutive man with a flat face answered the door. He was dressed like a servant, but I noticed that his hands were soft and manicured and his shoes were far more expensive than could be acquired on a servant's salary.

Frank told the man in unaccented German that we had urgent business with the countess. It was imperative to the Fatherland that we speak with her immediately.

The man examined us and then slowly relented, opening the door wide and ushering us into an elegantly decorated parlor.

"Excuse me," he croaked in a harsh voice. "I will tell the madam that you are here."

In a few minutes he returned with a tall, regal-looking

woman in her fifties. She wore a long ivy print silk dress with two large pockets at the hip and clung to a matted mink stole. Her nails were painted red.

"I am the countess," she declared a bit uneasily. "What is it that you want?"

I noticed that her servant continued to loiter in the room.

"May we talk to you alone, ma'am?" I asked.

The countess glanced nervously at her servant and wrung her hands. "Oh, Hans is always with me," she explained. "I have these fainting spells and cannot be left alone. He is quite deft at catching me when I fall."

"Perhaps you could sit," I suggested.

The countess slid a sideways look at Hans and then nodded slowly. "Perhaps I could," she concluded, taking a seat on a divan by the fireplace. She waved her jeweled hand at the servant. Was it shaking? "Hans, you may go."

Hans stood a moment, flustered.

The countess looked at him and spoke again, this time more firmly. "Hans, you may go."

The servant turned and exited the room.

I immediately confronted our hostess. "Countess," I asked, "are you being held against your will?"

In a hushed tone, the countess explained what had happened. She had agreed to tell Joe all she knew about the nutcracker, but moments after he arrived, the SS had stormed her home, taking Joe captive and keeping her prisoner in her own house!

"We must get out of here," Frank declared. "And fast!"

"You're not going anywhere!" a voice growled. It was Hans the servant, only now he was wearing the black uniform of the

SS, and he had three other officers with him. His gun was pointed at us, and he grinned maliciously. "Miss Nancy Drew and Mr. Frank Hardy," he drawled. "I've read about you."

"Almost none of that stuff is true," I explained quickly.

"No time for that now," he interrupted.

The three of us were marched upstairs to the attic of the house, where we were bound and gagged!

"You want to be reunited with your brother?" he asked Frank. "Here he is." Hans opened a small door to an attic storage closet, and Joe, bound and gagged, rolled out onto the floor. "Our plan worked perfectly," Hans laughed. "We knew that if we held Joe Hardy captive, his more experienced older brother would come to his rescue. And who else would he ask to accompany him but the attractive teen sleuth, Nancy Drew? Our intelligence has known for years that the Hardy Boys and Nancy Drew are the West's greatest weapon against us. It was our chance to get rid of all of you at once!" Hans picked up a can of gasoline and began to pour it on the attic floor. "It's funny," he added. "I thought that you would be younger." He lit a match and threw it.

The room immediately began to fill with smoke and flames. Hans and the other Nazis had left us to a ghoulish fate! What a turn of events! I wiggled furiously against the ropes that bound my hands and feet but could not loosen them, and I could see that Frank and Joe and the countess were failing to free themselves as well. The smoke grew thick and I began to cough and gasp for oxygen. The flames were only a few feet away!

Suddenly, the attic door flew open and a man came running in. He had a blanket and began to douse the flames with it. In several minutes, the fire had been extinguished. The man then ran to a window and used his elbow to break the glass so the smoke could clear. As it did, I recognized the mysterious stranger.

It was Ned! My own Ned!

Ned quickly untied us and removed our gags. "I think we're safe for the meantime," he announced. "Burt and Dave have subdued the Nazis downstairs." Burt Eddelton and Dave Evans had both been friends of Ned's since college.

"But how did you find us?" I asked.

Ned explained that he had run into Cherry Ames in Chicago and quickly realized that he had been duped. He immediately contacted Bess, who reported seeing what she believed to be a dirigible behind the Hardy house moments before we disappeared from the funeral gathering. Ned called Burt, who worked at the War Department, and Dave, who was unemployed, and together they put together the pieces and quickly commandeered passage into Berlin.

"Well, I for one am glad you did!" I exclaimed, beaming.

"But what about the nutcracker?" asked Frank.

Joe chimed in. "The countess was just starting to tell me when the Nazis burst in."

We all turned to the countess. "My great-grandfather was the Russian jeweler who made the nutcracker," she began. "He was a frustrated mathematician and he developed a code that could not be broken. The nutcracker is hollow. The code is inside."

"And now it's in the hands of the Nazis!" Frank fretted.

The countess smiled. "My grandfather thought that something like this might happen. So he made two nutcrackers.

One was sold to a rich fat man in Zurich. The other was kept in the family." She stood up and walked across the attic and pressed a panel of wood on the wall. A door sprang open, and the countess removed a parcel wrapped in cloth. She unwrapped it. It was the nutcracker!

"The Nazis almost burned it right along with us," Joe marveled, shaking his head.

The countess placed the precious nutcraker in my hands. "You take it now," she told me. "Take it, and let us hope that it does some good in ending this war."

Two weeks later we were all again gathered in the large, comfortable Hardy living room.

"So how did you ever get out of Germany?" Laura Hardy asked, amazed.

"It's a long story," Frank laughed.

Joe Hardy sat between his mother and his wife, Iola, on the floral print sofa. Mrs. Hardy squeezed his hand. "I'm just glad you're okay," she smiled.

"So what now?" asked Fenton Hardy.

"Well," I responded, "Burt is going back to the War Department. Dave is joining the Merchant Marine. Frank is going back to Washington, Joe will get his next assignment in a few weeks, I suppose, and Ned and I are going to move back to River Heights."

"River Heights? Really?" Frank asked.

"Ned and I were talking on the sub ride back," I explained, my eyes dancing. "And I think it's time he got out of the meat-inspecting business. Everyone needs life insurance, especially during wartime, and my father knows people at R.H. Mutual.

Besides, River Heights is a really nice town. And a great place to start a family," I winked.

"Why, Nancy!" Laura Hardy exclaimed.

The men stood to shake Ned's hand, and Frank gave me a courtly peck on the cheek. "Congratulations," he whispered. He put his face close to ear. "For what it's worth," he told me, "I wish it were mine."

I forced myself to smile graciously. I had spent the last few weeks confused and elated, guilty and jubilant. I had never imagined myself as a mother, but I wanted this baby more than anything. I loved Frank. But the country needed him, and who knew how long the war would rage on, or what danger he might face before it was over? Ned could offer me stability in the form of a brick colonial and a new roadster every year. My own Ned.

I glanced at him now, beaming at me with pride, and then at Frank, who had stepped back into the shadows. I did not know what the future would bring. But one thing I did know was that Ned would never find out what went on in that hayloft.

IV THE MYSTERIOUS MRS. DREW, 1944

Ned Junior wailed beside me as I sped to my father's downtown River Heights office, leaving a cloud of dust and gravel in my wake. When my father, the handsome, world-famous attorney Carson Drew, had phoned and asked me to come by as soon as possible, I had, in my haste, nearly driven off with Ned Junior on the hood.

I adored Ned Junior. He was like a stolen heirloom and a secret treasure all rolled into one. But sometimes when I looked at him he reminded me of all that I was missing. I resented him. And this consumed me with guilt. Some mornings, I had difficulty getting out of bed. Today my symptoms might be diagnosed as postpartum depression. At the time, doctors called it "organ neuroses related to the uterus."

It always helped to get out of the house, and by the time I finally sat across from my father it was all I could do to contain my delight. "This better be important, Dad!" I scolded, bouncing the shrieking titian-haired tot on my knee. The truth was I was thrilled that Dad had called. It had been years since he had asked me to help him out with a mystery! I crossed my fingers that it might involve the Amish. I so loved a good Amish mystery!

My father folded his hands on his large desk. "Nancy," he declared, "I know you've been blue since Ned Junior was born. You've taken less interest in household chores and rarely go to Burk's, Taylor's, or even Hidelberg's on shopping sprees. You haven't recovered a stolen purse or decoded a message in years. I'm worried about you. Mrs. Gruen and I are both worried about you."

Hannah Gruen, the housekeeper who helped raise me, still worked for my father as a maid and part-time secretary. She made my father call her Mrs. Gruen, though to the best of anyone's knowledge she had never been married.

My father continued. "We think that your, um, difficulties with motherhood may trace back to your own lack of maternal influences." He cleared his throat. "I know that I've led to you believe all these years that your mother was dead . . ."

With the instinct of a detective who dared not miss a clue, I begged him to continue.

"Your mother did not die of influenza, or in a fire, nor was she attacked by a collie." (I had always been fearful of collies.) "Your mother ran off. She was a suffragette."

"Oh!" I cried.

I should take the opportunity to clarify another murky point of Carolyn's making. I was not ten when my mother "died," as Carolyn first wrote. She later revised my age to three, which was correct, but not before her factual lapse had led to many embarrassing encounters when strangers would be surprised to learn that I had no memory of the woman they thought had died when I was an adolescent.

"It was 1913. Your mother had been volunteering with several women's charities. She had worked on behalf of orphans and the enslaved peoples of the world and against habit-forming tonics. She had campaigned for Woodrow Wilson and raised money for a ladies' auxiliary hall, and she began to get ideas about voting. She never did forgive me for voting for Taft. She wanted to join a suffragette march on Washington. It was to take place the day before Woodrow Wilson took office. I forbade her to participate. She left me the next morning." His eyes filled with tears as he gazed at his folded hands. "I told everyone that she had died. You have to understand that these were different times, and I had a fledgling law practice to protect."

"She's still alive?" I stammered, still in shock at the surprising news.

"I don't know," he sighed. He took a faded newspaper clipping out of his pocket and laid it before me on his desk. "As you know, being a world-famous attorney requires extensive business travel. I was in Los Angeles several years ago and came across this photograph in the Hollywood *Daily Citizen*."

I glanced down at the photograph. It was a picture of a crowd of mourners lining the street after the famous silent film star Rudolph Valentino died. I whipped my magnifying glass out of my purse and leaned forward to scan the faces in the photograph under the glass. My heart jumped. There was my mother. She had bobbed her hair and traded in her corset for a black flapper dress and opera shoes, but I recognized her immediately from the one small portrait my father still kept in the house. She was one of a throng of thousands, her face stricken, her eyes very large and sad.

"There she is," I whispered.

My father cleared his throat. "I felt it best to protect you from this. It was so long ago and we have moved on with our lives. But now I realize that we can't move on as a family until we put the past to rest behind us." He rested a hand on mine and squeezed. "I'm not alone anymore."

"I know," I told him. "You have me."

He coughed. "No. I, uh, I mean that I've found someone. A lady."

I froze. "Excuse me?"

"You know her. Marty King."

"Your twenty-four-year-old, platinum blond research assistant?" I asked incredulously.

"And recent graduate of nearby Bushwick Law School," my father added.

"She's going to be my stepmother?"

Ned Junior began to cry again. I held him close and rocked him on my lap, feeling his tears seep into my sweater set.

"I need you to find your mother," my father instructed. "For your own sake. And also for mine. I never had her declared legally dead. If she is alive, I need to get a divorce so that Marty and I can marry. When you were a teenager you would sometimes help me with my cases, and I always valued your counsel and keen mind. This could be your most challenging mystery to date." His gaze was pleading. "Will you help me?"

My mother had not died when I was three. There had been no rabid collie. She was out there. Somewhere. I was thirty-four years old, but for a moment I felt as if I were sixteen again. I could feel the dark cloud of the last several months lift, replaced by the marvelous sensation of a puzzle waiting to be solved. It was a sensation I had not felt in many years.

"I must find her!" I exclaimed, wiping a tear from my cheek. "I must find my lost mother!"

A deep sigh of relief escaped my father's lips. "If anyone can do it, you can!" he declared. "I have complete faith in you."

My eyes sparkled with anticipation. My very own mother and a new mystery, all rolled up in one. I had always found that missing mothers made for particularly enjoyable cases. Now who could I get to take care of the baby?

George Fayne answered the door with a gasp of surprise. "Nancy, what are you doing here?"

My tomboyish chum was still working as a riveter down at the River Heights docks. She lived in an apartment on Cottage Street near the warehouses on the wrong side of the tracks. It was an area of town where many young women with short hair and boys' names lived.

I excitedly told George about my new mystery.

"Hypers!" she exclaimed.

George's roommate appeared in the doorway from the bedroom they shared. Her name was Victoria, but she preferred to be called "V." A short, brawny girl with some Cherokee blood, V also worked as a riveter. I didn't know much about her except that she enjoyed motorcycles, arm wrestling, and herbal tea. I had always thought her a bit queer, though an excellent bridge partner.

"Hello, Nancy!" V growled amiably.

I repeated my story to V as she listened in amazement. "So," I finished, "will you watch the baby? Will you watch Ned Junior while I embark on this new adventure?"

"What about your husband?" inquired V dubiously.

"He's taking his life insurance exams in Omaha," I explained.

George cracked her knuckles thoughtfully and glanced at V. V nodded. "Okay!" cried George. "We'll do it! When do we start?"

"Right now?" I suggested.

"But Nancy, you don't have the baby with you."

I glanced around the apartment. They were right! "Oh." I smiled, chagrined. "I must have left him in the car. In all the excitement."

I retrieved Ned Junior from the roadster, handed him over to George, and caught the next Federal flight west.

The Federal DC-3 landed at Los Angeles Municipal Airport, and as I descended the staircase onto the tarmac, I was greeted with a blast of bright desert heat. I made a mental note to quickly change out of my chic fitted wool suit and extremely large hat. I retrieved my smart blue luggage and headed to the bank of phone booths in the adobe-style terminal. Fretfully, I skimmed through the Los Angeles city telephone book looking for my mother's name. I did not hold out much hope of finding it so was not terribly surprised when my search yielded nothing. Undaunted, I searched the listings under R until I came to what I was looking for: the Rudolph Valentino Fan Club and Remembrance Society. I dropped a nickel in the pay slot with a gloved hand and dialed.

A fat, cheery female voice answered. She did not recognize my missing mother's name but told me that the group would be having its monthly meeting the very next night and that I could address the group with my query. Perhaps someone else would remember a woman fitting my missing mother's description, she suggested brightly. I got an address, thanked the woman, and hung up just as a ruckus broke out in the terminal.

An elderly gentleman had collapsed!

Other passengers immediately began crowding about the fallen man, asking silly questions and generally getting in the way as I rushed to his side. Luckily for him, I was able to elbow my way through. He was a dapper little fellow clad in a coffee-colored suit with patch pockets, a blue silk shirt, and a coffee-colored tie. His gray hair was combed back straight from his forehead, and his face was ashen. I knelt beside him and felt for a pulse. It was weak.

"Someone find a doctor!" I cried to the throng of onlookers.

"I'm a nurse," exclaimed a voice. "Can I help?"

The crowd parted and I looked up to see a slender, healthy, and well-built young woman with very dark hair that glistened against the sharp white of her nurse's uniform. I groaned inwardly. *Cherry Ames.*

"Hello, Nancy," purred Cherry as she approached me with the famous proud erect posture that made her seem beautifully tall and slim.

"Cherry," I exclaimed evenly, trying to mask my dismay at the sight of my nemesis. "What are you doing here?"

Cherry shook her dark curls cunningly. "I'm an army nurse," she retorted. "I've just returned from Washington, where I have been personally attending to a very famous general."

I'll bet, I thought.

The man groaned. Cherry regained her nurse's composure and got to work. She ordered a big, sandy-haired woman in

"I'm a nurse," exclaimed a voice. "Can I help?"

the crowd to fetch a glass of water. When the woman returned, Cherry threw the water in the man's face. He sputtered and regained consciousness. The crowd applauded. "That elderly gentleman is alive because of her!" someone in the crowd shouted. "That nurse is a hero!" Others in the group muttered their agreement.

The man sat up groggily. "What happened?" he asked.

"You fainted," Cherry told him authoritatively. "I'm a nurse."

He blinked a couple of times as if to clear his head and then glanced about, embarrassed. "I must have had a few too many highballs on the flight from Washington. Please don't tell anyone about this," he pleaded, getting to his feet. Then, without even saying thank you, he picked up his suitcase and darted off into the crowd.

"What a strange elderly gentleman!" observed Cherry.

"Yes," I agreed.

We exited the airport, and I reached into my purse for cab fare, anxious to part ways with Nurse Ames.

"You'll never get a cab!" Cherry scolded. "They always pick up the servicemen first. Why don't you let me give you a ride?"

I stole a look at my black-haired companion. While the notion of spending time with Cherry gave me pause, I thought that carpooling was the least I could do for the war effort, so I agreed.

Cherry had a canary yellow 1939 Plymouth convertible, which she drove at an alarming speed toward my hotel. She had graduated from nursing school only the year before and was still very much delighted with her accomplishment.

"Nursing is the most rewarding of all professions for women," she informed me. "And frequently the most romantic and exciting."

"It must take a special kind of person," I commented, imagining a life of making beds and emptying bedpans.

We passed small adobe-style houses and Spanish-style architecture as well as modern sandstone office buildings. Even then the air hung heavy with haze, and the city seemed to shimmer with heat. I had to squint to see the low hills that squatted to the north and east.

Cherry yammered happily about her most recent doctor crush and spoke animatedly about the Brown Derby and other city hotspots that she frequented with her fast nurse friends. She had been stationed in Los Angeles for five months and found it far preferable to her hometown of Hilton, Illinois.

I suppose I told her about my missing mother in an effort to get a word in edgewise. I immediately wished that I hadn't as she became convinced that she could be of help.

She moistened her lips thoughtfully. "I don't have to report to work for another day," she exclaimed. "Why don't you bunk with me and we can go look for your mother together?"

I hesitated. I had always enjoyed solving a mystery with a chum, but Cherry Ames?! She would sell her own twin brother for a nurse's watch and a pair of white, rubber-soled shoes. Still, I knew that if I were going to find my missing mother I would need the help of someone who knew the city.

"All right," I agreed.

Cherry lived in a small stucco house in Inglewood with two other girls who worked as night shift nurses at Los Angeles

General Hospital. She had one bedroom, and the other two girls shared the other. The house had nice furniture and bright yellow curtains on every window. I recall that it smelled vaguely of formaldehyde. Cherry's roommates were asleep, so Cherry and I played gin rummy and smoked Chesterfields until it was late enough to drift off.

The next morning, Cherry took me on a short tour of the city. We saw the ocean, the oil derricks, the orange groves, muscle beach in Santa Monica, and Gary Cooper's house. I wanted to see Clark Gable's house in Encino, but Cherry refused. We fought bitterly. Then it was afternoon and time for the monthly meeting of the Rudolph Valentino Fan Club and Remembrance Society.

The Society met in a Spanish-style villa in the Hollywood Hills. The home was the private residence of the club founder and president, Mrs. Eugene Boil. An enormous woman with an equally large voice, Mrs. Boil answered the door herself and ushered us back to the parlor where the group was already gathered. (I had explained my predicament over the phone, and Mrs. Boil had agreed that I might come to the meeting and ask the members if anyone remembered my missing mother.)

The society had been formed in 1926, shortly after Valentino died of a stomach ulcer at the age of thirty-one. At its height, there had been 231 members. Now, including Mrs. Boil, there were exactly five. They were all generously built women in their late fifties with the gossipy demeanor that the happily widowed often possessed in those days. I explained my presence and passed around the yellowed newspaper clipping of my mother at Valentino's funeral.

"Did this woman ever come to your meetings?" I asked.

The women examined the clipping through their spectacles and pursed their lips thoughtfully in unison.

"Why, she takes evens," one of them declared.

I could feel my stomach tighten. "What does that mean?" I asked.

Mrs. Eugene Boil stepped forward authoritatively. "Part of our club charter stipulates that a bouquet of roses be left on Rudy's grave every year on his birthday. We partner with another club, the Rudolph Valentino Society of Admiring Friends. We do odd years. They do evens."

Cherry groaned audibly. I shot her a quieting glare.

"So my mother is part of this other club?" I asked Mrs. Boil. "You've seen her?"

"Well, yes, dear. Now that I see the photo, I recognize her too. She is the founder, president, and only member of the Society of Admiring Friends."

I swallowed nervously. "Do you have her address?"

"Of course," Mrs. Boil declared defensively. "We have to coordinate florists, don't we? But she doesn't go by Constance Drew anymore. She uses the name Connie Drawn."

Mrs. Boil walked over to a bookshelf and pulled down a large leather ledger. She opened it, leafed through the pages, and finally held it out for me to see. There it was, as big as life:

Connie Drawn. 44 Vine Street, Apt. #3

"Thank you," I cried gaily.

We sped directly there in Cherry's convertible. I could barely speak I was so overcome with emotion. This did not stop

Cherry from babbling incoherently about a whole host of subjects that had mostly do to with boys. Finally, we arrived. The building had been built in the twenties and surrounded a courtyard with a pool that had long ago been drained.

I rushed to apartment 3 and knocked.

A middle-aged gentleman answered the door. He had bristly hair and was casually dressed in brown slacks and a white undershirt. He looked mildly amused.

"Where's the fire, cupcake?" he asked.

"Fire?" I shouted. "What?!" I had been well trained in fire extinguishing and rued my lack of bucket. I was preparing to sling the man over my shoulder and carry him to safety when Cherry took me by the shoulders.

"There's no fire," she explained. "The bum's just trying to be cute." She turned to the gentleman and poked him hard in the chest. "So listen, bub, I'm a nurse, see? This dame's looking for her missing mom. Do you know Connie Drawn, or what?"

The man dismissively waved a hand. "Connie Drawn hasn't lived here in months," he retorted.

"But she did live here?" I asked excitedly.

"Yeah. With a couple of Orientals, Ai and Ko Sato. Then they got hauled away, and I guess she split too, 'cause next thing I knew, all three of them were history."

"They were arrested?" I asked.

"Naw," explained Cherry. "They were interned, right?"

The man nodded.

"Which camp, do you know?"

"Manzanar."

"They got internships at a company called Manzanar?" I asked, confused.

The man widened his eyes and looked at Cherry. She sighed and shrugged.

"Thanks, bub," she told him, dragging me by the hand to the car.

"We've got to find out more about this internship program," I declared when we got back in the car.

Cherry's jaw tightened. "There's no internship program," she explained slowly. "The government is housing the Japanese at camps on the West Coast. Manzanar is where a lot of the Japs from L.A. are sent."

"Why, Cherry Ames, that's the most ridiculous thing I've ever heard," I chortled. "Why would the government send the Japanese to camp?"

"They're internment camps," Cherry flashed impatiently, "not summer camps. It's like jail. Prison. The big house. They lock them up. Get it?"

"But why?"

Cherry's eyes narrowed. "Why, for their own protection, of course."

I was still puzzled by this but had the greatest of faith in the reasoning and actions of the United States government. "We have to go there," I declared. "We have to go to Manzanar and talk to that Oriental couple who lived with my missing mother."

Cherry looked over at me, clearly very pleased with herself. "That's the crazy thing," she retorted slyly. "You know my new assignment, the one I start tomorrow?"

"Yes."

"I'm going to be an internment camp nurse. I'm to report at Manzanar first thing in the morning!"

★ ★ ★

Manzanar consisted of row upon row of tarpaper-covered wooden barracks of simple frame construction, surrounded by a barbed-wire fence. It was in the desert, northeast of Los Angeles, at the base of the rugged eastern Sierra, where summer winds billowed fine sand continuously over the barren landscape. I had never seen anything quite like it, with the exception of a girls' camp I had been sent to as a child. I had not liked that camp either and had quickly, out of boredom, uncovered a plot to kidnap one of the counselors. The entire camp was immediately closed down so that local law enforcement could investigate.

Cherry showed her papers and identification to the soldier at the gate.

"Who's the blond?" he asked, jabbing a finger toward me.

"I'm not blond," I politely corrected him. "My hair is titian."

He surveyed me coolly. "Whatever you are, you aren't going inside unless you've got papers saying you've got clearance."

Cherry bit her bottom lip and fluttered her thick black lashes flirtatiously. "Can't she come in just for a minute? To help me get settled?"

The solider turned a deep scarlet. "All right," he agreed gruffly. "But just for a minute."

Cherry's quarters were in a shed near a barbed-wire fence at the back of the camp. The only furniture was a cot with a brocade bedspread, a potbelly stove, and a small dressing table. Cherry was to work three double shifts, during which time she would live at the camp. The rest of the week she planned to live in Los Angeles.

"Wait here," ordered Cherry. "I'll report in at the main office and see if I can find out which barracks the Satos are in."

I sat down on the cot and organized my purse. By the time I was done Cherry had returned with two files.

"Here they are," she exclaimed brightly. "Ai and Ko Sato."

I opened up the files, which contained basic information about each individual along with a black-and-white photograph. My gaze fell on the photograph of Ai Sato. She wore traditional Japanese garments, and her dark hair was pulled into a bun at the base of her neck. But I still recognized her.

"That's no Oriental!" I shouted. "That's my missing mother!"

It did not take me long to piece together what had happened. My mother was in love with Ko Sato. When the threat of internment was raised, she began disguising herself as Ai Sato, so that if he was taken to the camps, she could go with him. And now, if I confronted her, I would reveal her secret and she would be made to leave her true love. But I had to see her! I decided that I would just walk through her barracks, in hopes of catching a glimpse of her. Then Dad could follow up with divorce papers by mail. In a place like this it was probably a real treat to get letters.

A few minutes later, clad in Cherry's gleaming white uniform so as to appear inconspicuous, I glided through the longhouse in which my mother now lived. Most of the barracks were subdivided into family units. In my mother's barracks, four childless couples shared one of these areas. There were no plumbing or cooking facilities, just a large, empty, wooden room with a stove and standard army steel cots around the perimeter. A few dressers, homemade curtains, and a wall calendar did not go very far to make the space homey. It was the middle of the afternoon so the camp's residents were out and about playing kickball in the sand and writing sad letters to Roosevelt. One elderly woman sat on a cot.

I stole a look at the cots assigned to the Satos and was surprised to see the bedding stripped and the mattresses rolled up. A trunk sat between the two beds.

"They're gone," the elderly woman muttered.

"Gone?" I asked.

"They escaped last night. She said you would be coming. She left that for you."

I fell to my knees in front of the trunk. I had been so close! Now my mother was gone again. Vanished. But this time she had left me something. Slowly, apprehensively, I opened the trunk. Inside, neatly stacked and well thumbed, were the first nineteen Nancy Drew Mystery Stories. My mother did love me! She had kept track of me in her own way. She was proud of my sleuthing. She knew about Ned and Bess and George and Hannah Gruen and all of the other people who had come into my life only to be parodied by Carolyn Keene's poison pen. On top of the books was a note. It read:

Dear Nancy,

I have enjoyed reading about your adventures. I am in love with an Oriental. We are heading north. Tell your father to declare me dead. I still think he should have voted for Woodrow Wilson. (Follow your heart.)

Love,

Your mother, Ai Sato

I had just finished reading the note and was folding it up to put in my pocket when Cherry Ames burst in, followed by four camp MPs!

"That's her!" Cherry shouted. "She stole my uniform!"

I was quickly arrested.

What a queer development, I thought as I sat on a hard bench behind bars.

"Hello, Nancy."

I looked up as Cherry Ames sashayed through the door. She was wearing her spare nurse's uniform and cap, and she looked particularly rosy cheeked and smug.

"Can you give us a minute?" she asked my guard seductively.

"Uh, sure," the young guard stammered as he quickly exited.

Cherry approached the bars, clutching her woolly white sweater around her shoulders.

"Why?" I asked.

"I have my own series now," she announced icily, black curls bouncing. "Thanks for mentioning it, by the way. I really appreciate your support." Her eyes went through me like knives. "But who wants to read about an adventuring nurse when she can read about a teenage detective? There's a nurse shortage right now, you know. It's a war job with a future. If my books can inspire little girls to go into nursing, then it might help us win this thing. But no! Everyone wants to read about a sixteen-year-old, uptight, self-centered, control freak daddy's girl. You couldn't earn a cap if your life depended on it! By tomorrow all the papers will know that Nancy Drew was arrested! Don't you get it? If I can discredit you, your book sales go down, and mine go up." She flared her nostrils patriotically. "Then maybe the Allies will stand a chance."

The door flew open, and the young guard came back in along with a diminutive, elderly gentleman who turned out to be the camp director. Cherry's and my jaws dropped. It was the gentleman who had collapsed in the airport!

The young guard walked past Cherry, took out a great set of keys, and opened the door to my cell. "You're free to go, Mrs. Nickerson."

Cherry's rosy cheeks paled. "What? You're not going to arrest her? She stole my uniform? She snuck into the camp!"

The camp director smiled amiably. "After what you girls did for me in the airport, I wouldn't dream of pursuing this. Besides, we decided that we shouldn't bring any extra attention to our internment project here. We don't really like publicity." He turned to me jauntily. "Mrs. Nickerson, may I drive you back to town?"

"Uh, sure," I replied. I was still very shaken by the day's events. I had found my mother only to lose her again. Could I count this case as solved, or would it skew my percentages? Even more pressing, why did my heart ache with such sorrow? I supposed it was the mother thing. There would be no tearful reunion. She had made her choice. She had chosen true love with an Oriental over me. Yet her note and the books made me believe that I inhabited a place in her heart. She could leave me—and love me. It was all pretty complicated. Then, the most amazing thing happened. Standing there in that internment camp jail, I felt something for the very first time: I felt like a mother.

I followed the camp director out of the building into the slanted light of the desert's setting sun. How I suddenly missed

River Heights! As we were leaving the camp jail, he turned back to Cherry. "Nurse Ames," he called over his shoulder, "there are some children projectile vomiting in Barracks Two. You better report for duty."

V THE SECRET OF THE AGED HOUSEKEEPER, 1953

"Nancy, I'm worried about you," commented Hannah Gruen, putting down her dish towel long enough to stand looking at me with her gnarled, fisted hands on her hips. Hannah had grown quite elderly, and as her helpfulness to my father diminished along with her stature, so did her house-keeping opportunities elsewhere. When Dad remarried, Ned and I agreed to take Hannah in. I loved her dearly and had come to think of her as family. Of course the arrangement was contingent on some light household chores.

Ned Junior was ten now and quite active. A student at the prestigious River Heights Laurel Leaf Girls' School (they had made an exception and accepted him in part due to my fund-raising efforts), he excelled at academics and field hockey.

"What an odd thing to say," I exclaimed to Hannah.

"You just don't seem yourself," Hannah muttered.

I examined my reflection in the kitchen window. I was still attractive, my hair as titian as ever (I had recently cut my bangs), my eyes a sparkling blue, but my perky cheeks had slackened and my eyes were lined with crow's feet. Even though I was still slim, I must confess that I had noticed that my skirts were fitting me a little tightly around the waist. "Whatever do you mean?"

61

"It seems as if you're avoiding your husband. You don't enjoy cooking. Or cleaning. You barely garden."

"Oh, Hannah," I smiled. "That's silly. You're talking about last weekend. I couldn't go to Ned's office party. I had to rescue Ned Junior from the old well in the backyard."

"But how did he get in the well?"

"I lowered him. We were playing 'rescue from the old well.'"

Hannah untied her cotton apron and sat down across from me. "There's something I should have told you a long time ago."

My ears perked up and I looked at Hannah with rapt attention.

"I knew your mother."

"You did?" I exclaimed.

"She was my sister."

My head felt light as I motioned for her to continue.

"Yes," she went on. "In addition to being your faithful housekeeper, I am also your aunt. Your father and I thought it best you never know the truth. We thought it prudent that she be pushed from your mind completely, to spare you a similar fate. Your father suggested that I work for free as a maid in your home. I agreed. But now I see that we made a terrible mistake. We should have been honest with you. I was the one who warned Ai Sato that you were coming to Los Angeles. If I hadn't, she might not have vanished forever, and you might have had your tearful reunion. Then perhaps you would not be smothering your sweet bastard son while ignoring your household chores and your devoted, hapless husband."

"You know?" I stammered.

"He is the spitting image of Frank Hardy."

I felt a crashing wave of relief flood over me. I had been so consumed with guilt over my deception that I had let my anguish eat away at my relationship with Ned, unable to qualify my overwhelming love for my son with my affection for my youthful sweetheart. Was it possible that, in my effort not to repeat my mother's mistakes, I had overcompensated? Then it struck me.

"You're my aunt?"

In the heat of the rippling revelations, I must admit that my detection skills were dulled. In most cases I would have heard the anxious footsteps quickly approaching the back door. As it was, I was as surprised as Hannah when the back door fairly flung open and eleven armed men stormed our comfortable home.

They surrounded my housekeeper/aunt, lifted her to her feet, and handcuffed her.

"Mrs. Hannah Gruen," one of them announced sternly, "you're under arrest. For being a Communist spy!"

Willing myself to remain calm, I phoned my father and told him that our housekeeper had just been taken into custody to appear before the House Committee on Un-American Activities. I did not tell him about Hannah's revelation. Then I phoned Ned at River Heights Mutual. Within fifteen minutes, both Ned and my father were sitting in our living room, my father still wearing his judge's robes.

Excitedly, I relayed the shocking events that had taken place during their absence. I cannot say why I chose not to reveal Hannah's stunning disclosure, except that at the center of my being I feared its volatility. As the keeper of my own astounding secret, to which Hannah was privy, I knew well the noxious gas

63

that lurked in untruths and I pledged silently to contain it. Or maybe I was just chicken. "Well," I asked, "what should we do? We just have to prove that Hannah is innocent!"

My distinguished father looked grave. "This is serious business, Nancy," he stated. "I'm not sure that any of us should get involved until we know what's really going on."

"But Hannah's no Commie!" I pleaded.

Dad shook his head grimly. "She never talked politics in front of you. But she was very progressive. She supported unions for coal miners."

Ned, now a vice president at the life insurance company, sat up tall in his smartly tailored sharkskin suit. He wore his hair handsomely slicked back and favored colorful ties. "You know I'd love to help," he offered consolingly. "But this sort of red scare could really hurt the business. Maybe it is best if we just keep this cat in the bag."

My eyes burned as I steadied myself on the davenport. "Okay," I agreed slowly. "We wait to hear the specific charges."

Ned stood and kissed me on the cheek. "Where's the little guy?" he asked, looking around, a flicker of concern in his eyes. "You weren't playing 'trapped in the old well' again, were you?"

"No," I answered. "He's upstairs. Reading."

Ned bit his lip. "Maybe I'll go ahead and take him into the office with me for the rest of the day. You seem excitable."

"Fine," I retorted.

I waited for Ned, Ned Junior, and my father to leave the house before I flew to the phone. I dialed the number I had memorized so many years before.

"Hello?" a voice answered.

My pulse raced as I gripped the receiver to my ear. "It's me," I gulped. "I need you."

"I'll send someone to pick you up," replied Frank Hardy.

I packed only the essentials: lipstick, rouge, foundation, mascara, eye shadow, eye liner, cold cream, curlers, a hairbrush, a magnifying glass, two pairs of stockings, two pairs of pumps, three pencil-straight skirts (two with elastic waistbands), four fitted blouses, a cashmere cardigan, two boxy jackets, an assortment of undergarments, and a bottle of Estée Lauder Youth Dew. Then I waited by the back window.

It was about forty-five minutes later that I saw the light in the sky and watched the three-decker plane soundlessly lower itself vertically into our backyard. No sooner had the great silver craft come to a stop then a blond, lanky young man leapt out of the plane and dashed to my back door.

"I'm Tom Swift Junior, ma'am," he exclaimed, extending a hand. "Frank Hardy sent me."

"I'm Nancy Drew," I greeted him. "I knew your father."

Once we were aboard the Sky Queen, Tom introduced me to his adventuring companion, a husky young flier named Bud Barclay. The two youths set the plane on gyropilot and offered to show me around the flying laboratory. Bud, who had the well-built, supple body of an athlete, led the way, while Tom explained the various purposes of supersensitive electronic controls and levers.

"So how do you know Frank?" I asked Tom.

"Well," Tom explained, "I was back at Swift Enterprises— our gleaming four-mile-square compound of modern facilities and airstrips—working on a method of using an alcohol–liquid oxygen fuel combination designed to absorb the hyper and powerful radiation of the sun and shoot this solar energy into the liquid oxygen supply, converting it into highly explosive, poisonous rainbow liquid ozone. I had just juiced up the electromagnets and was in the process of lowering them into the acid vat full of electric eels, when who should walk through the door but Frank! He said that the government needed my experiment. On the double. So of course I handed it over, no questions asked. How about you?"

I became very interested in a nearby gadget. "Oh, I helped him find a missing waitress once," I replied, shrugging.

"Hey, watch the thermograph potentiometer!" Tom cried alertly, pulling me away from the instrument I had been fingering.

I hurried to catch up with Bud, who had climbed into the transparent blister above the pilot's compartment.

"This is the astrodome," Bud explained, proudly gesturing to the view.

It was a remarkable vista. Nothing like commercial air travel. I could see for miles in every direction.

"Is that Washington?" I asked, pointing to the skyline we were approaching.

"Yep," answered Bud. "We should be safely on the ground at the naval air strip shortly. I'd better return to the landing instruments. Tom will want to activate the patrol scope before we descend."

Fifteen minutes later, the sliver-winged laboratory had landed and we had all been quickly ushered into an underground hangar. A young uniformed man led us down a series of well-lit hallways until we came to a closed, unmarked door.

"You can go in," he declared.

I suddenly found myself consumed with self-consciousness. I had not seen Frank Hardy in eleven years. I was forty-three years old. Would he still find me attractive? My face burned with embarrassment at my schoolgirl awkwardness. What a fool I was! I had abandoned my romantic hopes years before. Sentiment and passion had no place in the life of a middle-aged wife and mother. I gathered my senses, smoothed down my titian tresses, adjusted my brassiere, and with a determined nod to Bud and Tom opened the door. It was some sort of conference center. A large table surrounded by chairs sat in its center. Maps of the world papered the walls. Sitting with his hands folded at the far end of the table was the love of my life, Frank Hardy. He stood when I came in. His hair was graying around the temples and he had a mustache, but I noticed that his tailored uniform fit crisply over his still strapping physique. A small tremble snaked its way from my ankles to my knees.

"Major Hardy," I purred, despite myself. "How nice to see you again."

Frank smiled. "Now what's this I hear about Hannah Gruen?" he asked.

Tom and Bud and I sat down at the table, and I told Frank everything I knew, including Hannah's familial confession. He nodded thoughtfully and several times consulted notes that he had laid out on the table.

"Nancy," he commented, "let me be straight with you. Hannah Gruen is a highly skilled Soviet agent bent on selling our most precious atomic secrets to the highest bidder."

I gasped.

"Just kidding!" he exclaimed.

He cleared his throat and continued. "Actually, Hannah is no spy. She was a member of the Communist Party for three weeks in 1913. But why the House Committee on Un-American Activities would choose to go after an elderly housekeeper for a youthful indiscretion, I don't know. They refuse to share their files with the military, but I can't imagine that they have any information that we don't." He looked up at me meaningfully. "I can only theorize that there is some dastardly plan at work here."

"Like that time when we were drilling for molten iron at the South Pole with the atomic blaster?" asked Tom boringly.

"Something like that," Frank answered, nodding.

"What are we going to do?" I asked.

Frank's eyes steeled. "We're going to go straight to the top."

We took Tom's four-person atomic-powered scooter straight to the White House, and moments later we were sitting in the Oval Office across from President Eisenhower. Frank relayed the situation.

President Eisenhower nodded. "I'll make some calls, Major Hardy," he offered. "But before I do, I should tell you that I think I already know why HUAC had targeted your Hannah Gruen."

"You do?" I gasped.

The president pursed his lips grimly. "In 1915, I was a second lieutenant stationed in Fort Sam Houston, Texas. I fell in love with two women. One of them I married. The other, a young suffragette in town to campaign for the vote, was named Hannah Gruen."

"Jumpin' jets!" exclaimed Bud.

The president continued, his face reddening. "I think that my enemies discovered my relationship with Miss Gruen and decided to charge her, knowing that I could not let our relationship come to light."

"What are we going to do, sir?" queried Frank.

"What my enemies want me to do," the president lamented. "I have no choice but to resign."

"You can't!" Frank gasped.

"Good night!" exclaimed Bud.

"It's not fair!" Tom cried darkly.

"Just wait a minute, Mr. President," I remarked. "You're saying that this is all an elaborate scheme to force you to step down as leader of the free world?"

The president nodded curtly.

"And that the only evidence they have that Hannah is a Communist is the fact that she was a party member for three weeks in 1913?"

He nodded again.

"So if those records were to disappear, then they would have nothing? And a youthful affair with a suffragette is far less harmful politically then an affair with a Communist."

The president considered this. "They probably wouldn't even go public with that," he mused.

"Mr. President, sir," I declared, "I ask that you give us twelve hours."

The president met my eyes with resolve. "Twelve hours, Mrs. Nickerson." He looked us all up and down, a flicker of apprehension behind his deep-set blue eyes. "I hope that you are as good as the books say you are. For all our sakes."

Back aboard the Sky Queen, hovering fifteen-thousand feet above the Capitol, Frank, Bud, Tom, and I considered our options.

"All right, gang," Frank declared, "let's go over this again. Who would stand to benefit the most from Ike's resignation?"

"Russia?" offered Bud.

"The Netherlands?" Tom asked flatly.

"Richard Nixon," I declared.

They all looked at me. "Think about it," I continued. "Who's to benefit directly? Eisenhower resigns. His vice president takes office. Richard Nixon. He used to be a member of the Un-American Activities Committee. He's arranged this whole thing."

"Which means that he's bound to have the evidence under lock and key in the vice presidential residence!" Frank gushed. "The only safe in the residence is in the first-floor den."

"We could use my hydraulic jackscrew!" Tom suggested inventively.

"But how do we get in the house?" mused Bud fretfully.

Tom's eyes lit up. "We don't," he declared. A broad smile spread across the face of the lanky young inventor. "We send a robot!"

As soon as night fell, we huddled in Tom's atomic-powered hovercraft on a quiet street near the vice presidential residence and set about recovering the evidence that could force a presidential coup.

Tom's eyes lit up. "We don't. We send a robot!"

Tom manipulated the robot using two levers on an instrument panel inside the hovercraft. A binocular camera was mounted on the robot's head, allowing us to view its progress on a monitor. The robot was two feet tall and had two extendable arms on each side of its boxy torso.

"It's the first robot ever powered by Swiftonium," Tom explained mechanically. "That's the radioactive isotope we discovered in South America. Of course, his shell is made of Tomasite, for heat resistance and to absorb gamma rays, but I've taken the extra step of covering the Tomasite with a coat of black Swiftonite paint, so the fellow can move unnoticed at night through populated areas." As if to illustrate his point, we watched on the monitor as the robot passed several Secret Service agents who remained unaware of its presence.

The robot approached the front door of the residence, and we watched entranced as it reached an extendable arm up, picked the lock, turned the doorknob, and entered the home of the vice president of the United States. We breathed a collective sigh of relief when the robot was safely inside, only to have that sigh turn to a gasp when an enormous racket exploded over the speakers on either side of the monitor. Tom expertly spun the robot around to face the source of the noise. We all immediately recognized Checkers, the Nixon family's cocker spaniel, who now stood snarling and barking at the invading robot.

"Quick," Frank demanded. "Steer the robot into the den before someone comes to check on the dog!"

With lightning reflexes, Tom guided the machine from the foyer to the den, using an extendable arm to quickly shut the door behind him, locking the crazed canine in the hallway.

"Nice job, old man!" complimented Bud.

"We're not done yet," Tom cautioned.

Our eyes were glued to the monitor as Tom guided the robot over to the wall safe behind the desk. Frank knew about the safe from the day he had come to the residence to break the news to Truman that Roosevelt was dead. Truman had removed some important papers before Frank drove him to the White House.

"The reception is good enough to activate the sonic interferer," Tom announced. He pulled a lever in the hovercraft. "That should absorb the noise of the hydraulic jack." He manipulated several other controls, and the robot retrieved the jack from its hollow body and began drilling into the lock on the safe's door. After several long moments, the door swung open. Tom activated a penlight on one of the robot's arms, and we examined the contents in the safe on the grainy monitor. We could see a metal lockbox, several bundles of Cuban pesos, and a stack of files. The top file was labeled "Hannah Gruen."

"That's it!" I exclaimed.

Tom directed the robot to pick up the file and insert it and the jack into its torso compartment. With steady motions, he guided the machine back to the hallway, past a wall display of framed photographs of Tricia and Pat, around the corner to the foyer, and back out the front door, just as Checkers, alert again to the intruder, came scrambling from his resting spot at the base of the stairs.

We waited until we were all safely aboard the Sky Queen to examine the file. Inside was a Communist Party meeting log that showed that a Miss Hannah Gruen had attended three party meetings in 1913. Affixed to the log with a paper clip was a smiling photograph of Hannah Gruen and Dwight David Eisenhower at the 1915 Sam Houston Sweetheart's Dance & Rodeo.

Frank used the Sky Queen's radiotyper to send a coded message to the White House, informing the president of our success. A few minutes later, the instrument picked up and decoded a response.

"What does it say?" demanded Bud.

Frank read the message aloud: " 'Good job, team. Leave the rest to me.' "

"What do you think he's going to do?" I asked Frank.

"They should lock Nixon up!" Tom suggested arrestingly.

Frank looked thoughtful. "If I know the president," he murmured, "he'll find a way to turn the tables on Nixon. It may take years, but he'll find a way to make sure Nixon gets exactly what he deserves."

Tom, Bud, and Frank flew me home in the Sky Queen. Tom and Bud stayed below in the pilot's compartment, and Frank and I rode in the astrodome.

"Back to River Heights," Frank declared.

"Yes," I replied.

"How is Ted?"

"Ned."

"Sorry."

"He's fine. He's a vice president now at R.H. Mutual."

"And your son?"

I reached up and smoothed a piece of Frank's dark hair into place underneath his jaunty army cap. "He looks just like his father," I whispered. My voice caught and I turned away. "Sometimes it breaks my heart to look at him."

Frank's voice was small. "I ought to be getting back. The president needs me."

I gave him a brave smile. "It's what I love about you."

Tom poked his blond head into the astrodome. "I'm afraid the wind's too strong to land," he announced. "We'll have to lower you down." I held Frank's gaze for a moment longer and then followed Tom down to the bay of the craft, where the young scientist lowered me with a swaying magnetic cable into dark expanse of my own backyard.

I could see my father and Ned through the kitchen window as I approached the back door. Hannah Gruen would be home soon. My own true aunt. (Eloise Drew, my supposed spinster aunt who lived in New York City, was a complete fabrication constructed by Carolyn Keene. In fact my father was an only child.) I used to think that I had not lived enough. I had a few great summers pursuing mysteries as a teenager, and I had been chasing them ever since. It was at that that moment, standing in our backyard looking at my family behind the glass, that I finally accepted that those summers were over. One morning you wake up and realize that the world has moved on. It was time to grow up. It was time to stop sleuthing and embrace my life as a mother and as a wife. Perhaps, I told myself, embracing domesticity would prove to be my greatest adventure yet.

It turned out to be my most harrowing.

VI THE MYSTERY OF THE
CONGOLESE PUPPET, 1959

"This is strictly dullsville," my pretty chum Bess Marvin
sighed, adjusting the Moroccan tunic she had brought back
from the trip to Tangier that had followed her third divorce.
"Dig?"

"Dig?"

"Hoo-boy, Sister," Bess exclaimed. "You're one real gone
chick." She stretched out on my davenport and went back to
reading *Exodus*, which she had just been assigned to condense
for *Reader's Digest*. Bess's perceived weight problem, thanks to
Carolyn Keene's character assassination, had led her to a life
spent trawling for men in search of affirmation. Her most
recent husband, a beatnik poet, had abandoned Bess at a North
Beach coffee house after telling her that she had been "weigh-
ing him down." He had immediately gone on to publish a
well-received chapbook of poetry titled "*Pretty, Plump Blond.*"
Still heartbroken, Bess flew to River Heights after her trip to
Tangier and had been staying with us for almost six weeks. Fast
approaching fifty, Bess held stubbornly to her youth and had
coped with her breakup by adopting the jive talk of the current
youth culture. It was getting on my nerves.

"I have no idea what you just said," I sighed, returning to
my dishes.

Hannah Gruen had died two years before. Though I had

77

investigated her demise in great detail for several months, even I had to admit, finally, that it was due to natural causes. She had kept my secret to the end. And I had kept hers. What's more, per my backyard promise, I had committed to the life of a dutiful housewife. I was not good at it and was often distracted by my ongoing pursuit of missing socks and waylaid keys. My greatest memories of those days revolve around a missing hamster. Sadly, we did not recover him alive. But it was still thrilling.

The back door burst open and in flew Ned, followed closely by teenage Ned Junior. Their clothes were caked with mud and their eyes were wild. My back tensed reflexively at their approach.

"Wipe your feet," I cautioned.

Ned grinned excitedly. "I think we're making real progress!"

He and Ned Junior had been building a bomb shelter in the backyard for several months. Ned had gotten it in his head that I wanted one after I had made a passing comment after reading an article in *Ladies' Home Journal* about the A-bomb. He could not be dissuaded.

"That's nice, dear," I remarked.

"Want to see the fallout minibar we built?" Ned asked, eyes bright. "If you huddle under it, it doubles as protection against atomic radiation. I painted it blue, your favorite color."

The phone rang. I picked it up and immediately recognized the urgent voice of my father, Carson Drew, the world-renowned attorney-turned-judge-turned-losing-city-council-candidate. While he had grown more wizened, he maintained his healthy spirits.

"Nancy!" he croaked. "Can you come over right away? I've come across something you'll want to see."

I hesitated only for a moment. "Sure, Dad," I agreed, with a sideways look at the Neds. "I'm on my way."

I sped to my stately childhood home behind the wheel of my blue 1958 Ford Ranch Wagon. I had traded in my latest roadster two years before, after Ned decided that it wasn't practical for a woman my age. I checked my appearance in the rearview mirror. My hair had started to gray and I now dyed it. At first I had tried blond, but it didn't suit me, so I had finally gone back to titian. I had grown accustomed to my aging features. I was still a handsome woman. My breasts were just a little lower and my hips a little wider. Cherry Ames, I happened to know, had gotten quite fat. Beside me, Bess twirled a piece of her silver blond mane and looked bored in the passenger seat. She was tanned and bedecked with beaded jewelry from her travels. I envied her freedom, if not her insecurities.

The house was the same as it always had been: a comfortable, three-story brick Colonial with a large front yard planted with rosebushes. How many eavesdroppers had we caught behind those rosebushes over the years? How many times had my father's study been burgled? But now a moving van sat outside. I stared at it gloomily. I had lived the happiest days of my life in that house. Now my teenage years would finally be truly lost to me. The acute passage of time seized me with despair.

Bess, seeming to sense my difficulties, straightened up. "Well, are we going to make the scene or what?" she demanded.

I sighed and tried to think of something pleasant like hula hoops and coonskin caps. "Let's go," I replied, forcing a smile.

My stepmother, Marty Drew, née King, and I had never gotten along, though I had made an effort to remain civil toward her. Now she had convinced my father, who was retiring, to sell my childhood home and move to Flagstaff to be closer to her relatives.

When Bess and I walked inside, we found my spacious, comfortable former home stripped of the belongings I had known and instead stacked full of moving boxes. Even the mantel, always a focal point of the living room, was bare. Marty had sold the old clock, fan doll, and ivory charm that I had displayed there since high school at a garage sale a few weeks before.

My father, still distinguished looking though far less handsome, approached us from the living room with an excited expression. He was slightly stooped and his hair had thinned to just a few wisps that seemed to tremble independently of his movements.

"Hello, girls," he wheezed. "You'll never believe what came in the mail."

He led us to the kitchen, where a strange wooden figurine sat propped next to the electric refrigerator.

"What's the beef, Daddy-o?" asked Bess.

"It's a Congolese puppet," my father explained. "A nice one, if I'm not mistaken."

"Where did it come from?" I quizzed him.

"It was delivered yesterday." He paused. "It was addressed to your mother!"

"My missing mother?" I asked, momentarily taken aback.

"Yes. To Constance Drew."

"Far out," exclaimed Bess.

I examined the puppet and the open packaging that lay beside it. There was no return address. The postmark indicated that it had been mailed from overseas. But my mother had not gone by the name Constance Drew in more than thirty years.

"It's a pretty nice puppet," my father commented.

"What am I supposed to do with it?" I asked. My enthusiasm wavered. "It looks hard to clean."

"I don't know," my father shrugged. "Take it home? I'd take it, but Marty says there's no room in Flagstaff."

The puppet, carved out of ebony, was in the shape of a laughing man. It was dressed in tribal finery and looked quite old. It wasn't really my style, but I thought it might look nice displayed in the new bomb shelter, so I stowed it carefully in the back of the station wagon. I admit that I allowed myself a small thrill at the notion that some small relic had been saved from Marty.

Once it was safely tucked away in the wagon, we said goodbye to my father and started home. We had just turned off Center Street onto River Drive when I noticed that we were being followed by a handsome, blond, well-muscled young man in a black Jaguar.

To confirm my suspicions, I made a quick turn onto River Lane, past Riverside Hospital. The black Jaguar was still behind us!

I doubled back and pulled into the hospital parking lot. The Jaguar followed.

"Where are we going?" Bess asked, sitting up. "Are you sick? Is it your cholesterol?"

"I think we're being followed," I explained. I watched the young man get out of his car and stride purposefully toward us. "And I want to see what he wants."

Bess's eyes widened.

I placed my hand lightly on the car horn, so that I could attract help if needed, and watched as the young man appeared at my window. He was wearing a slim, dark suit and wore his blond hair stylishly feathered. He smelled faintly of hair spray.

"Nancy Drew," he declared. "I'm Christopher Cool, TEEN agent."

"You're a teen agent?" I asked.

"Actually I'm twenty. I work for TEEN, the Top-secret Education Espionage Network. We're so top secret the world won't even hear about us for another ten years!" He grinned affably. "I'm a sophomore at Kingston U."

"Never heard of it."

"It's Ivy League," Chris replied defensively.

"Why are you following us?" I asked.

"That's classified, I'm afraid."

"What do you want?"

"We want the puppet."

Bess leaned forward. "I dig your skinny tie," she purred.

Chris Cool's cheeks flushed. Though Bess was nearly fifty, she could easily pass for forty-five. "Thanks, ma'am."

My head was spinning. How did he know about the puppet? Why was it so valuable? And what did it all have to do with my mother?

"What does TEEN want with a Congolese puppet?" I stammered.

Chris looked uncomfortable. "So you know it's Congolese?"

"It's obvious to anyone who knows anything about sub-Saharan folk puppetry," I answered smartly.

"Both of you and the puppet are going to have to come with me," Chris ordered, brushing a blond forelock off his forehead in frustration.

"Okay!" exclaimed Bess brightly, hopping out of the car.

"If we come with you, will you explain what this is all about?" I asked.

Chris sighed. "I'll do what I can," he promised.

We left the station wagon in the parking lot and took Chris's Jag to the River Heights temporary TEEN headquarters, located in the basement of Wishing Well Shoes. The room was empty except for a small oak table and a dark-haired young man with high cheekbones and obsidian eyes. He stood when we entered.

"This is my Apache Indian roommate, Geronimo Johnson," Chris announced, introducing us.

"Your roommate?" I asked, arching an eyebrow.

Chris cleared his throat. "At school."

Bess heaved a small sigh of relief.

The Apache glanced at Chris with humor in his eyes. "You were just supposed to bring back the puppet, *choonday*."

"They know it's Congolese," Chris explained.

"So what's this all about?" I demanded steadily.

"Better get TEEN Control on the phone, Gerry," Chris barked to his roommate, ignoring me.

Chris's youth was charming, but his manners weren't. "I thought his name was Geronimo," I observed.

Chris bit his lip. "It is Geronimo. Gerry for short."

"You could try to be a little more respectful of his Apache heritage," I suggested.

"I am respectful!" Chris exclaimed.

Geronimo nodded thoughtfully. "You know, she's right," he agreed. "I do prefer my full name."

"You've never said anything," Chris floundered.

"You never asked."

They stared at each other in stony silence.

"So listen, what's the deal with the puppet?" I tried again.

Chris sighed. "I just know that we're supposed to recover the item and report with it to the River Heights airport." He raised his head slightly. "It's a matter of extreme international importance."

Bess slid next to Chris, pressing her ample, if slightly sagging, bosom against his chest. "So, if you're twenty, when do they let you join the real CIA?"

Chris took a small step back. "TEEN is a unit of the CIA, ma'am. And it is an honor to serve my country as a TEEN operative."

"I'm sure it is," Bess whispered huskily.

"I demand that we be taken to your leader," I announced.

"Excuse me?" Chris's eyebrows shot up in alarm.

"Your boss. The head honcho. The big enchilada. I am a citizen and my personal property has been confiscated and I want to speak to the man in charge."

Chris swallowed hard. "Please, ma'am."

"I am Nancy Drew," I declared, "and I smell a mystery." My blue eyes flashed. I may have been middle-aged, but I was still a teen sleuth at heart. "About such things I am never wrong."

TEEN HQ was located on a secret floor of the Luxury Motors Building on Broadway and Fifty-sixth Street in Manhattan. We flew to New York, where we picked up another black Jag and drove to the building's service garage. Chris and Geronimo led us through several checkpoints, past several men with submachine guns and several pretty secretaries, until we were face to face with a man sitting behind a massive walnut desk. He looked like a crazed yacht enthusiast: blue blazer, yachting cap, unlit pipe, grayishblond beard.

"Your boss is a sea captain?" Bess inquired of Chris skeptically.

The man rose from behind his desk, his face red and sweating. "What is the meaning of this?" he growled in a decidedly fake British accent.

I stepped forward. "I am Nancy Drew," I explained, "and I demand to know what you want with my puppet."

The man's angry expression melted immediately. "*The* Nancy Drew?" he asked.

"Yes," I replied, flustered.

He picked up a book and came rushing around the desk. "Will you sign a book for my granddaughter?"

"Of course," I cooed, opening up a copy of *The Hidden Staircase*. To whom shall I sign it?

"Katherine."

"With a *K*?"

"Yes."

"What's going on?" broke in Chris.

The man's face flushed again as he glared at the TEEN agent. "You mean to tell me that you don't know who Nancy Drew is?"

Chris looked as if he was about to cry.

"She is only the original teen sleuth. The prototype. The inspiration for this whole business."

"They had teen sleuths in the twenties?" asked Chris, confused.

Chris's boss ignored him and stepped forward, thrusting his hand out toward me. "I'm Q," he declared. His lips peeled in an effort to smile. "It is an honor and a pleasure, madam."

I introduced Bess. She vamped nervously.

"Now that we all know whom we're dealing with, Q," I continued, "how about telling me what exactly you and TEEN are up to?"

"Of course," Q stated. "We traced the puppet from Leopoldville, the capital of the Belgian Congo. It was mailed by an associate of Patrice Lumumba's. Belgium, as I'm sure you know, is losing control of the Congo at an alarming rate. We suspect that the Belgians will grant the Congo independence this summer and that Lumumba will be elected prime minister. Because Lumumba has Communist ties, the CIA has an interest in transitioning control of the country to someone more"—he searched for the word—"amenable. We want to know why the puppet was sent and what significance it has."

"What do you suggest?"

"I plan to send Kingston One and Two here to the Congo with the puppet, where they will confront Lumumba."

"But it's my puppet."

"Surely you recognize the importance of this mission."

"Of course." I took a step forward. "That is why I want to go," I declared confidently. "Send me, Mr. Q. Send me to the Congo."

"What?" cried Chris and Bess in unison.

Q's face lit up. "Fantastic! I was hoping you'd offer. A sleuth of your stature would be welcome. Of course you'll have to take Kingston One and Two here with you. It will be good training for them."

Chris paled. "You want us to take orders from her?" he inquired, glancing over at me dubiously. "She's old."

"I'm experienced," I corrected him.

"What about me?" Bess asked. "Can I come?"

"You must come!" I urged, already excited by the prospect of an international caper.

Bess gazed seductively at Chris. "I so enjoy the company of young people," she purred.

We flew with the puppet by military transport to Leopoldville. It was the middle of the night when we touched down. A red Jaguar was waiting in the airport parking lot with the keys in the ignition.

"Shouldn't we have a jeep or something?" asked Bess.

"I always drive a Jaguar," barked Chris. "We'll want to go straight to the meeting place," he added, shaking the wrinkles out of his suit jacket. "Give the boys a heads-up, Gerry— Geronimo."

Geronimo nodded, expressionless. "Do you want me to use the wristwatch communicator or the radiotelephone, oh wise white man?"

Chris sighed deeply. "Will you just stop it?" he demanded.

"Injun so sorry, Kemo Sabe."

"We'll talk about this later."

"Red man very patient."

"Stop it."

"Come on, Nancy, let's you and I ride in back," suggested Bess. We got in the Jag and Chris took the wheel and Geronimo climbed into the passenger seat.

Chris steered the Jag out of the parking lot and onto a quiet highway that led into the countryside. After twenty minutes we pulled to a stop outside a small tarpaper shack. A light was on inside and I could see movement.

"Do you have a zip pen that fires anesthetic barbs?" Chris asked me.

"Uh, no," I answered.

Chris looked concerned. "A fraternity pin with an adrenaline hypo?"

"No."

"What do you have?"

I lifted my heavy magnifying glass out of my purse. "This."

He raised an eyebrow skeptically. "Let's go," he declared. "The Indian and I will watch your back." He turned back to Bess. "You stay out here behind the wheel in case we need to make a quick getaway."

"It's because I'm fat, isn't it?" Bess asked accusingly.

Chris looked confused. "No."

"It's okay," Bess allowed. "I understand if you're embarrassed."

"You're not fat," Chris told her emphatically. "At all. We just need someone in the car. Behind the wheel. In case we need to make a quick getaway."

Bess blushed. "You can count on me."

When we got to the door, Chris rapped on it three times in quick succession. It opened slowly, and a tall African man dressed in a black suit appeared. He was carrying a submachine gun. He ushered us into the room. Two more men stood leaning against the wall, their guns hanging casually from their hands. Another man, clearly the leader, sat at a small table. He was wearing gray pants and a leopard-print tunic.

"Colonel Joseph Mobutu," Chris Cool stated flatly.

Mobutu smiled broadly, his white teeth a startling contrast against his dark skin. "Christopher Cool," he declared. "The cool cat himself. The big daddy. The wolf man."

"I need a favor."

"I will do anything I can to help TEEN."

"I need to find Patrice Lumumba."

"What makes you think I know where Lumumba is?"

"Because he is your enemy. And you are a smart man."

Mobutu laughed and waved a finger playfully at Chris. "You are pretty smart yourself. For a teenager."

"I'm twenty," Chris insisted through clenched teeth.

Mobutu glanced over at me. "I know who the Indian is, but who's the schoolteacher?" he asked.

I stepped forward. "I'm Nancy Drew."

His eyes widened in recognition. "I am reading *The Mystery of the Tolling Bell*."

"Any good?" I asked.

"It is very exciting." He looked at Chris and then at me and back again. "I'll tell you what you want to know. But then TEEN owes me a favor."

Chris nodded slowly. "Yes."

Mobutu gave us directions to a church in Leopoldville where Lumumba was said to be preparing his independence movement. We drove there in silence.

When Chris pulled the car to a stop outside the stone structure, I cleared my throat. "I think I should go in by myself," I offered carefully.

"It's too dangerous," Chris replied. "You're fifty. You're out of shape. You don't even know aikido."

"I can fake it," I assured him. I got out of the car before he could protest again and, carrying the puppet in a burlap bag, walked quickly to the side door of the church. It was unlocked, so I entered. The door opened onto a stairway that led to the church basement. I closed the door behind me and descended the stone stairs. At the bottom of the stairs, another door led to a hallway. At the end of the hallway was another door, this time open. I entered it. A bearded African man with horn-rimmed glasses stood waiting for me.

"Lumumba," I greeted him.

"Nancy Drew," he replied, nodding.

"You knew I'd come?"

"I knew that you would come looking for who had sent the puppet."

"It was you, then?"

"No."

"Then who?"

"You have met Mobutu?"

"Yes."

"He is a bad man. Our colonial days are coming to a close. The country will be in chaos. Mobutu seeks to profit from our misery both in power and in riches."

"I think I should go in by myself," I offered carefully.

"And what do you seek?"

"The only thing I want for our country is the right to a decent existence, to dignity without hypocrisy, and to independence without restrictions."

"And the puppet?"

Lumumba approached the bag, opened it, and withdrew the puppet. Then he twisted off the puppet's head and poured the contents of the hollow skull into his cupped hand.

"Diamonds!" I exclaimed.

"They are Mobutu's stolen bounty. They were stolen from him three weeks ago."

"By?"

"By a TEEN agent called Spice."

"Why would a TEEN agent called Spice steal Mobutu's diamonds?"

"To make him think that I did."

I was still having trouble following. "You're accusing a teen sleuth of having acted unethically?"

"I know that this will be hard for you to hear," he declared gently, "but the CIA has been manipulating teenage agents for years. It was clear from your exploits and those of the Hardy brothers that teenagers were capable of great sleuthing. The CIA immediately put a program in motion that would train teen agents to carry out government actions. That program became the Top-secret Education Espionage Network. They know that Mobutu is a fan of yours, and now he thinks that you also work with TEEN. He has heard that the puppet was sent to you. Because you went to him and asked him how to find me, and knowing that you are an ace sleuth, he now thinks that I stole his diamonds and sent them to you to get them out of the country. He will stop at nothing to destroy me. Just as the CIA planned."

I was stunned. Was it true that I had been manipulated into upsetting this delicate power balance? I had once been in a very similar situation involving a circus ninja and an evil child soothsayer. I did not like revisiting it. "You must tell TEEN superagents Christopher Cool and his Apache Indian room-mate Geronimo Johnson everything that you've told me," I urged.

"It's too late for that." Lumumba sighed, shaking his head. "TEEN and the CIA believe that Mobutu will be an ally. I have too many friends in the Soviet Union. I can only delay the inevitable now."

"What about the diamonds?"

"They are fakes," he declared, straightening up and pushing the puppet into my arms. "Your friends have already returned the real diamonds to Mobutu. He grows more powerful as we speak."

"Chris Cool is a brilliant agent," I persisted. "I just know that he can help."

"Is he brilliant?" Lumumba muttered, with a faint, melancholy smile. "Then perhaps he will be the one they send to assassinate me."

There was nothing more to say.

Lumumba gestured at the door. "Go," he ordered. "You are in danger every moment that you are here. The rioting is going to start soon."

I backed out of the room and left him there. The grim look of futile determination on his face never left me. I ran all the way to the car, clutching the Congolese puppet to my breast.

Back at TEEN headquarters in New York City, I rushed into Q's office with Chris, Geronimo, and Bess on my heels. "Tell me it's not true!" I demanded.

Q sat with his hands neatly on his desk. His face was impassive. "Thank you for your help, Mrs. Nickerson."

The realization of my unwitting participation in TEEN's plan was a bitter pill. I shook my head sadly. "It is true."

"What's going on?" asked Bess.

I held the puppet out toward Q. "Are the diamonds in here even real, or have the real diamonds already been returned to Mobutu?"

"You should join the CIA," Q smiled. "You're very intuitive."

My blood was boiling. "You have to do something," I declared grimly. "You have to tell the truth about what happened. Tell Mobutu that Lumumba did not steal his fortune."

"You may go now," Q retorted.

"What's going on?" Bess asked again in a small voice.

I clenched my fists in frustration. "We were used," I told her. I gestured at Chris and Geronimo. "We were all used." I glared at Q, my jaw jutted out, my blue eyes on fire. "Adventures are supposed to be fun," I announced indignantly. "Finding a hidden message in a tapestry, recovering a lost inheritance, thwarting a kidnapping—these all make the world a better place. But what you do isn't fun at all. You manipulate world events. You take sides." I gave him my most accusing stare. "You're using TEEN to carry out the CIA's dirty operations, and in the process you're making a mockery of good, old-fashioned teen adventures. You, sir, give sleuthing a bad name."

I could see Chris stiffen, and Bess put a hand over her small mouth in distress.

Q raised a bushy eyebrow. "I should think you would be proud of all we've accomplished."

I shook my head in disbelief. "If the CIA ever needs help tracking down a lost locket, give me a call. Otherwise I never want to hear from you again." I thrust my chin out defiantly. "One more thing," I added. "If anything ever happens to Lumumba, I'll make sure that history knows who was behind it."

"Come on, Nancy," Chris broke in. "I'll take you to the airport."

I let him lead me out of the office.

"What about you?" I asked him once we were in the hallway.

He looked chagrined. "Things are a lot different from when you were young. Lying, assassinations, duplicity—it's just how the world is now."

"You plan to stay on with TEEN?" I was incredulous.

"Well," Chris replied, "I do have a school break coming up, and I was thinking of taking a vacation." He shyly reached down and took Bess's hand. "Would be you interested in accompanying me?" he asked her.

Bess's free hand fluttered to her chest. "You bet I would."

"You're jetting off on a vacation," I stammered, "when there is injustice and treachery in the world?"

"I'm Chris Cool," he sighed. "I won't even be declassified until 1967. So in the eyes of the world, none of this has happened." He put his arms around my shoulders. "That's another thing that's changed since your day. We've learned a lot about publicity." (I couldn't argue with that.) "Go back to River Heights, Nancy Drew," Chris urged, "and be glad that your teen sleuthing days are over."

I said good-bye to Chris, Geronimo, and Bess and flew home to River Heights alone, my spirits decidedly low. When I got back to our spacious ranch-style home, it had been two days since Bess and I had left to see my father. Ned was sitting on the sectional watching *Gunsmoke*. He didn't look up.

"The bomb shelter is finished," he told me quietly.

My soul felt empty and my hair felt flat. "I'm sorry."

"Where were you?"

"Africa."

He looked up at me. He had been crying. "You have to stop doing this. You can't keep disappearing for days on end without any explanation. What am I supposed to tell Ned Junior when you vanish without a word? He cried himself to sleep last night. I caught him cuddling with a copy of *The Clue in the Jewel Box*. Don't you care about us at all anymore?"

"Of course, I do," I sighed, sinking down on the sofa beside him. "It's just that sometimes I feel like I'm drowning. Like I'm trapped in one of those secret rooms and I can't get out." My heart filled with sorrow as I touched his familiar face. "I long for adventure, Ned. I want to fall down staircases and elevator shafts. I want to explore caves and wear disguises and be left for dead. I want to use my skills for good. I thought that if I ignored these longings, they would wither and die, but

96

they haven't. The last few years I've been trying to be something I'm not, and it has nearly destroyed us."

We were silent for a long moment and then Ned asked, "So what now?"

I considered this. "We take some time. We reevaluate."

He nodded, and I could see all of our youthful dreams in the reflection of his eyes. "I still love you."

"I love you too," I told him. But I wasn't sure I meant it.

VII THE HAIGHT-ASHBURY
MYSTERY, 1967

"Nancy, you did it again!" exclaimed Captain Tweedy admiringly, as he led away another shoplifter from Burk's Department Store. I smiled winningly and, with a self-effacing shake of my bottle-titian hair, retorted, "Just doing my job, Captain!"

I had been working as a store detective at Burk's for almost three years and had single-handedly apprehended more than five hundred shoplifters. In those days no one paid much attention to anyone over thirty, so as a woman in her late fifties, it was easy for me to follow suspects unnoticed. Despite my efforts, theft in the store continued to be a problem, as long-haired youths streamed through town on their way to counterculture hubs such as Indian City and Ann Arbor.

It had been six years since I had finally left Ned and Ned Junior. We had tried couples therapy, encounter groups, and even a Masters and Johnson seminar. In the end nothing had helped me overcome the feeling that I just didn't have what it took to be married. I had broken Ned's heart, and in exchange I granted him primary custody. He loved Ned Junior as much as I did, and in the end I could not bear to leave my devastated special friend alone. I eventually purchased the industrial flat that George had been renting out since she had left town in 1955 to get her doctorate at the University of Chicago. It was here I began my late-middle-age renaissance. I even bought a 5th Dimension album and learned how to macramé.

Ned Junior had graduated from Berkeley and chosen to remain west, settling in an area of San Francisco called Haight-Ashbury. Our relationship had been somewhat strained during his late teen and college years, as I tried to make a career in store detecting, but we had ultimately remained close. My analyst said that I had an unusual interest in people and situations that promised mystery and adventure, and that this led to trouble coping with the mundane activities of ordinary existence. He called it "teen sleuth syndrome" and even wrote a paper on it that was well received at several national conventions. The heart of the matter was this: I was obsessed by mystery. Because of this, I found it difficult to take time off from store detecting, which offered me a multitude of small capers in need of solving. As a result, though I spoke to Ned Junior often by phone, I had yet to visit him in California. George, who had always taken an interest in Ned Junior, became convinced that I should tear myself away from my job and surprise Ned Junior with a visit.

"There is more to life than shoplifting!" she had exclaimed over the phone. "And much of it is in San Francisco."

I liked the idea of a surprise visit. It seemed as if it might have the potential to be thrilling, while allowing me to be secretive and maintain an aura of mystery. I was also a little sore from being on my feet all day. So I agreed.

When my plane landed in San Francisco, I collected my old blue suitcase and got in line for a shuttle bus. As you may be aware, at that time San Francisco was a great gathering place for young people from all over the country. These young people grew their hair long and wore untailored, unironed clothing. While I had briefly encountered bohemian types shoplifting at Burk's, I was looking forward to experiencing the counterculture firsthand. I had stood in line only a few minutes when I was approached by one of its representatives.

"Hey, sister," asked a shaggy-haired youth behind me in line, "where are you headed?"

I told him the address of the house that Ned Junior shared with several other young adults.

His saucer-sized eyes lit up. "That's in the Haight, man. That's where we're headed." He shot a thumb behind him to three other bohemian-clad youths. "Do you have any bread?"

"Bread?" I asked.

"Money, man. 'Cause Jim has a van in short-term parking. We just don't have enough gas to get across town, dig? You throw in some bread and we'll take you to the Haight."

I climbed carefully into the back of Jim's red VW microbus, modestly adjusting my paisley skirt as I tucked my orthopedic shoes under my legs and took a seat on a stained mattress.

One of the two girls in the youthful company took a seat beside me, grinning widely. "I'm Starfire," she announced. "Jim and I have a pad together. Coyote, there"—she pointed to the shaggy-haired youth who had approached me—"just got back from five months in Europe."

I glanced at the other girl, a young teenager with a freckled face and short, sandy curls, who sat curled glumly against the door. "And who's that?" I asked.

Starfire shrugged. "Oh, that's Foxy. We picked her up hitching on the way here. She's from a farm in New York or

101

something." Starfire leaned a little closer to me. "There are a lot of runaways here," she confided.

Foxy looked up at me, her blue eyes flashing in defiance. Of course I would have known her pert nose and rolled-up dungarees anywhere. This wasn't just any runaway; this was Foxy Belden-Frayne, the daughter of Crabapple Farm's own sleuth, Trixie Belden.

The bus came to a stop at the corner of Haight and Ashbury. There was a great deal of activity outside. Young people in colorful dress filled the streets. A ragtag marching band was performing while a group of young women danced without their tops.

"There's some sort of parade," Jim informed me. "We're going to have to let you out here. Just walk a block that way." He pointed up a sloping hill.

I leaned toward Foxy. "Do you have a place to stay?" I asked.

She shook her head.

"You can stay with me." I held out my hand. "Come on."

She hesitated for a moment, then took my hand, and we climbed out of the bus into the Summer of Love.

"Do your parents know where you are?" I asked Foxy as we negotiated our way through the circus atmosphere of the Haight.

She clenched her teeth. "Jeepers, no!" she declared with a dismayed grimace. "They understand me about as much as a bobcat understands a copperhead!" She tossed her curls defiantly.

"Listen," I replied, "I've met your mother. She must be worried sick."

"I know I'm a goop," Foxy shrugged. "Moms and Daddy are tops, and Aunt Honey is the best. But sometimes a girl just has to get out on her own, you know?" Her blue eyes snapped with excitement as she surveyed the colorful people and shops all around us. "We just don't see this sort of thing in Westchester County."

We came to a tall Victorian that stood in some disrepair next to a noodle shop. A large banner with a peace symbol painted on it adorned the front window. I checked the address in my purse. This was it.

Foxy and I climbed the rickety steps of the house. The doorbell was not working, so I rapped on the oval window of the front door. In a few minutes, a bearded, long-haired young man appeared, rubbing his eyes. I recognized his ensemble as typical of the so-called hippie scene: blue jeans, an Indian-style shirt, a bandana tied around his forehead, and no shoes.

I put on my most dazzling smile. "Hello," I declared brightly, "I'm looking for Ned Junior. Please tell him that I have come to call on him."

The youth blinked several times. "Mom?" he asked.

I examined the youth for clues. His hair *was* titian. "Ned Junior?" I asked. "Is that you?"

He looked stricken. "What are you doing here?" he demanded.

"I wanted to surprise you," I explained. "I'm here for a week. Aren't you going to invite us in?" After seeing his long hair and beard, I understood why he hadn't come home that Christmas.

"Who's that?" he asked, pointing at Foxy.

"That's Foxy Belden-Frayne."

Foxy took a small step forward. "My mom's a pretty famous detective in Westchester County, New York," she explained. She blushed modestly. "And I'm not so bad myself."

Ned Junior swallowed hard and opened the door a little wider so we could enter.

That night we sat on the floor of the living room eating rice that one of Ned Junior's housemates had prepared with Ned Junior and eight other young people. They all eyed me suspiciously.

A grim-looking young woman wearing a black turtleneck and blue jeans sat down next to Ned Junior. I saw her jut her chin my direction. "Who's she again?" she demanded.

"My mom," Ned Junior replied.

The woman's brows shot up. "Nancy Drew?"

"Nancy Drew."

"Man," the woman declared, rolling her eyes, "that is so square."

Ned Junior bit his lip, eyes burning. His housemates continued to stare. "I really wish you'd called first, Mom," Ned Junior shared for the fifth time. "We have a lot going on this week."

I sat up. "Is there a mystery? Can I help find something for you?"

He sighed. "No, Mom. We're organizing a demonstration for free speech."

"You should plant clues all over the city that people could follow to the demonstration site," I suggested.

"No, Mom. It's not a scavenger hunt. It's a protest. We're expecting thousands of people."

"Any villains?"

He groaned helplessly. "Not like the ones you mean."

"Oh." I examined my bowl of rice sadly.

"You really miss it, don't you?" Ned Junior asked softly. "Amateur detecting."

I shrugged and put on my bravest face. "There just aren't any good mysteries anymore," I replied casually.

A tall, skinny youth in a cowboy hat and Indian caftan sidled up to Foxy. "So how old are you, anyway?" he asked.

"Fifteen," Foxy told him. "I'm a Junior Bob-White."

"What's a Junior Bob-White?" the cowboy asked, confused.

Foxy grinned indulgently. "Our super-special club, of course!" She slugged him playfully on the arm and he withdrew befuddled, rubbing the spot where she'd hit him. "Jeeps," Foxy whispered to me. "We'd never let any of these kids in the Junior Bob-Whites. I bet they couldn't birth a foal if the mare's life depended on it!"

I awoke early the next morning and rolled up my bedsheet from the place on the floor where I had slept next to Foxy and four strangers. The others were all still asleep, so I decided to go for a walk to get some air.

I left the house and headed down to Haight Street. It was early enough that the street traffic was sparse and many of the small shops had yet to open. I was standing in front of a clothing store, admiring a slimming blue skirt in the window, when I saw a reflection in the glass.

I spun around, and my heart rose in my throat. "Frank?" I asked.

Frank Hardy turned his head at his name and stood looking at me, jaw agape. He had a heavy beard and was wearing blue jeans, a blue work shirt, and large moccasin-style boots. He wore his graying hair in a short ponytail, tied with a thin leather strap.

"Nancy?" he muttered incredulously, his face creasing with delight.

I stepped forward and kissed him lightly on the cheek, liking the feel of his coarse full beard on my lips. "What are you doing here?" I asked. I glanced around. "Are you under-cover?"

He smiled, chagrined. "No. I left the service a few years ago. I run a free clinic down the street." He held out an arm for me to take. "Let me show you. I'm headed there now."

I took his arm and he caught me up as we walked. "It was Vietnam that finally woke me up," he told me. "Do you remember Tom Swift's friend Bud Barclay?"

I nodded.

"He was killed on a sortie just over a year ago."

"I'm sorry."

"Bud's death really got to me. I left as soon as I could. Moved out here. Opened this free clinic. We offer basic medical treatment for the kids in the area. A lot of drug overdoses, that sort of thing. We're all the help a lot of these kids get."

We came to a four-story brick building on a corner. "This is it," Frank declared.

He showed me around the clinic and then took me to a nearby vegetarian restaurant for lunch. We talked for hours about our lives. Frank told me that Joe and Iola had four children. Joe had stopped drinking and had taken over their father's private detective agency when Fenton had died of a massive stroke—no great surprise, given all of Aunt Gertrude's high-fat cooking—while investigating the Mystery of the Masseuse. I told Frank about Ned Junior and Senior and my longing for adventure. Frank had never married. I asked him why.

"It just never felt right," he explained.

"What about sleuthing?" I asked. "Do you miss it?"

He was thoughtful. "It's not our world anymore, Nancy." He sighed. "It's a lot more complicated out there than when we were young. Mysteries have changed. Villains today are not so black and white. And the technology is changing all the time. I'm content to leave the sleuthing to the next generation. Have you heard about this kid, Encyclopedia Brown?"

"But we can be updated," I insisted. "We can be brought up to speed. I just know that we still have a place in this world as sleuths. Just think how much more we know now than when we were sixteen!"

He smiled sadly. "People don't remember," he declared heavily.

"They do!" I insisted. "I'm recognized all the time!"

Frank put his hand on mine. "It was good seeing you," he muttered gently. "Now I should be getting to work." He slid his chair back from the table and stood up.

I felt a catch in my throat. "Do you want to meet him?" I asked. "Ned Junior?"

Frank was silent, his face a veil of regrets. Then, slowly, he shook his head. "I don't think I'm supposed to," he murmured.

He turned and walked away. Through the restaurant

window I watched him walk off, hunched, hands in his pockets, until he was out of sight.

When I arrived back at the old Victorian, the house was in an uproar. Ned Junior met me at the door, his face stricken. He was clutching a handwritten note. "It's Dad!" Ned Junior cried, his bearded face smeared with tears. "He's been kidnapped!"

I calmed Ned Junior down, and he and Foxy explained what had happened. Unbeknownst to me, Ned Senior had also planned a visit to San Francisco, for a national life insurance convention. Ned Junior was expecting him to arrive that morning by cab for a visit before proceeding to his downtown hotel. But when the cab arrived, Ned Senior was not in it. Instead, the cab driver brought a note to the door that he said a man in a hat and overcoat had instructed him to deliver. The note, handwritten on a white index card, read:

Send help. Beware the turtle. Dad

Foxy had grilled the cab driver for more information, but, satisfied that he knew nothing and could not describe the man in the hat with any accuracy, she let him go on his way.

"This is extremely mysterious," I observed.

Foxy nodded vigorously.

We sat yogi-style on the floor of the living room and went over our options. "He probably checked into the hotel before he came here, right?" I looked at Ned Junior.

Ned Junior said, "Yes."

"Okay. So that's where we start. Who has a car?"

The hippies looked around at one another helplessly.

"No one?"

They all shrugged.

"Ned Junior?" I pleaded.

"I have a motorcycle with a sidecar," he offered.

"Okay." I sighed. "Foxy and I will take that, because we are the most experienced at sleuthing and I know how to handle a chopper. All the rest of you find a car and get down to the hotel as soon as you can."

"Should we call the cops?" asked Ned Junior.

"In my experience," I explained, "the police should not be called until the very last minute."

The hippies all nodded in agreement.

"Okay," I declared. "Let's go."

At the hotel, we had to spend several minutes in the ladies' room while I restyled my hair, which had been whipped up ferociously by the wind on the ride over. Foxy did not seem to mind the state of her sandy blond curls, though I encouraged her to wash the dirt off her face, which she did. Once my bottle-titian tresses were combed so smooth they shone, we marched to the front desk.

"I'm Mrs. Nickerson," I declared pleasantly. "I seem to have lost the key to my room. I believe it's under my husband's name, Ned Nickerson, the famous life insurance agent?"

The balding man behind the counter gave me only a momentary glance before handing me a key with the room number stamped on it: 405.

Foxy and I proceeded to the fourth floor and down the hall to Ned's room. I knocked softly on the door. No one answered. I put the key in the lock and opened the door.

"Jeepers!" Foxy exclaimed breathlessly.

The room had been ransacked!

Foxy and I cautiously examined the damage. The mattress had been pulled off the bed. All the dresser drawers were upended. Ned's suitcase lay open, and all of his neat slacks and jackets were strewn about the room. It broke my heart to see all his tidily pressed plaid slacks and wide ties thrown into disarray.

Foxy was already on her hands and knees on the carpet looking for tracks.

"See anything?" I asked, offering Foxy my magnifying glass.

"There's been a scuffle," Foxy reported. "I see men's tracks all over the place. There were either several of them with roughly the same shoe size, or just one intruder who was a real wildcat."

A note on the bedside table caught my attention. I picked it up. "Look at this!" I exclaimed. It was another handwritten note on an index card. It read:

Room #204. Hurry. Dad

"I think this is a clue," I told Foxy.

She cocked her freckled face. "Do you think the gang of men with the same shoe size kidnapped him and are holding him two floors down?"

"Maybe," I mused.

"We should go check," she suggested.

"Yes," I agreed.

The hotel's second floor hallway was deserted. Foxy and I approached room 204 stealthily and with great haste. I placed my ear against the door. Nothing. I tried the doorknob. The door was unlocked. I pushed it open, and Foxy and I entered the dark hotel room, despairing of what we would find. We had taken only a few steps when we heard a terrible groan. Foxy threw on the lights.

Ned was seated on the floor tied and gagged! What dastardly villain was at work? I rushed to his side, kneeled, and untied the gag, while Foxy began cutting away at the ropes that bound his ankles with her pocketknife. I had not seen Ned in months and could not help but feel that had I been there for him, this might not have happened.

"What happened?" I asked him urgently.

"Don't know," he mumbled. "I walked into my room and saw a ghostly hand!" He grinned at us in a silly sort of way, then tried to stand up but sank to the ground.

"Are you ill?" I cried.

"I've been drugged. Chloroform. Or something equally powerful. I fought as hard as I could, but I couldn't breathe. Then I went out like a light. Didn't know another thing until I heard your voice."

"Wait a minute," I asked slowly. "Didn't this happen in that book Carolyn wrote, *The Ghost of Blackwood Hall*?"

Ned looked sheepish. "I thought you didn't read those."

My eyes narrowed. "I've read a couple. Just to see what all the fuss was about." I turned to Foxy. "Can you excuse us for a minute?"

Foxy's eyebrows shot up, but she did as I asked and walked out into the hallway.

"You faked this whole thing, didn't you?" I asked Ned evenly.

111

"What happened?" I asked him urgently.

Ned began to cry. "I saw you with Frank Hardy," he explained tearfully. "I was on my way to Ned Junior's in the cab and I saw you walking arm in arm with Frank. Seeing you with that Hardy boy made me realize how much I still loved you. I remembered how much you used to like to rescue me, and I thought that if I faked my kidnapping and you could rescue me again you'd realize how much you missed me. So I came back here, ransacked my room, disguised myself, and sent the cabbie with the note, and then I trussed myself up and waited for you to come." He sniffed. "I knew you would."

"What about the turtle?"

He grinned. "I just threw that in for a little color."

I put my hands on my hips and regarded Ned gravely. He had grown out his sideburns to a ridiculous degree. "You scared Ned Junior silly, you know. He's probably stealing a car right now so he can make it here to help find you."

"I'm sorry."

"And what about Foxy? You know that's Foxy Belden-Frayne out there in the hallway. Her mom's a pretty famous detective in Westchester County, New York."

"I'll apologize to her," Ned promised quietly.

"This was all for my benefit?"

He wiped a tear from his cheek with the back of his wrist and nodded.

Ned Nickerson. My Ned. My attractive, paunchy, balding, bumbling Ned. Even though I didn't feel that we should be married, I felt that we belonged together somehow. He was a good man. And he truly did love me.

"I can't be married to you," I told him. "It's not in my nature."

He nodded.

"But maybe we could try being special friends?"

His eyes lit up. "Do you mean it?"

"No pressures about marriage. No housework. No smothering."

"What about Frank?"

I thought about this. I loved Frank Hardy. I always would. But sometimes it was like we were from different universes, like our stories didn't entirely intersect. "I'm not meant to be with Frank," I declared finally. "I'm meant to be with you."

Foxy and Ned and I ran into Ned Junior and the hippies in the hotel lobby. They had indeed stolen a vehicle. It took us most of the afternoon to return the mail truck to the post office without detection and before the mailman realized it was missing. But that's another story.

VIII THE MYSTERY OF
THE SEVEN SISTERS, 1975

"Actually," I announced to the auditorium, "I think that books about girl sleuths should be an integral component of the feminist canon."

There was a smattering of applause in the audience and nodding from my panel mates. It was the first annual Female Protagonists in Young Adult Series Literature Feminist Conference at Vassar College, and George Fayne, now a distinguished, tenured professor and author of the book *Clitoris! Clitoris! Clitoris!* had invited me to participate. Others on the panel included Cherry Ames, who had recently been hired as a Teamsters nurse; Kim Aldrich, who was fighting the glass ceiling as a secretary for the international insurance firm WALCO, Inc.; and Judy Bolton, the attractive wife of an FBI agent, who had her own series of books, though they did not sell as well as mine.

A serious-looking young woman with very straight hair, no makeup, and wire-rimmed glasses raised her hand.

"Yes?" I asked.

"My name is Madge Hollings," she announced. "Isn't Cherry Ames a more important role model than you are, since she actually showed young girls that they could make their way in the world as working women?"

I paused. "I guess so," I allowed. "If you consider nursing

the pinnacle of female success." A shocked murmur ran through the crowd. I continued, "She can't even hold down a job. Dude ranch nurse. Cruise nurse. Private duty nurse. Army nurse. Rest home nurse. Ski nurse. One right after the other."

Cherry glared at me, her black eyes flashing. She had not aged well. Though she was younger than I was, her weight had ballooned, a fact that was not well disguised by her blinding white size-sixteen (and too-snug) uniform. I had heard that she was diabetic. "My skills were in great demand. That's what attracted Helen to my story."

I threw my hands up dramatically. "You always knew how to promote yourself, Cherry. That's why you started writing stories." I looked out at the crowd, waiting until I had all of their attention, before I dropped the bombshell. "Under the pen name Helen Wells."

The crowded gasped.

Cherry's chubby cheeks turned scarlet.

I surveyed the auditorium. "I bring this up only to show you that you too can make up your own stories. We are not slaves to the perception of others. We are each of us our own biographers. As young women today you are in a unique position. The obstacles are crumbling. The world is opening itself to possibility. Look for mystery behind every corner. And when you think you have it figured out, look closer and work harder, because the truth takes time and effort, but it is worth it. Thank you."

The crowd burst into enthusiastic applause.

George approached the microphone on stage. She still wore her hair short, though she had let it gray. Her features had grown more masculine as she had aged, a fact only highlighted by her lack of cosmetics and the fact that she appeared to have a fine mustache. She was wearing her uniform of black turtleneck, long macramé vest, and black slacks. "Thank you. Thank you, everyone, for coming. We'll see you all tomorrow for Donna Parker's lecture on girls and large horses."

As the young women in the audience stood and began to form a line to talk to the panel, out of the corner of my eye I saw Cherry waddle from the stage.

After the auditorium had cleared out, George, Kim, Judy, and I had dinner at a restaurant near the college. Cherry did not show. I regaled the threesome with stories of Ned Junior's courtship of Foxy Belden-Frayne, who had stayed in San Francisco and become a well-regarded record jacket artist. They had finally married the year before, and Foxy was pregnant with their first child. After dinner, George took us all back to our hotel and we said good night in the lobby. When I returned to my room, I called Ned and told him about my day. I took an Ex-Lax, as was my evening routine. Then I fell asleep.

It was nearly three A.M. when the phone rang. It was George. "You better get down here to Grover Hall right away," she declared urgently. "It's Cherry Ames! She's been murdered!"

By the time I had pulled on my control-top panty hose, corduroy skirt, turtleneck, blazer, and sneakers, styled my hair, applied tasteful cosmetics, and caught a cab to the campus, almost a dozen police cars had arrived at the crime scene. I ducked under the yellow crime tape and headed toward the door of the building. A uniformed police officer stopped me.

"I'm Nancy Drew," I explained. "The sleuth."

He looked me up and down. "Whatever, lady," he shrugged.

I whipped out my identification and presented it to him. He looked at it, then at me. "Shut up!" he cried. "You're real?"

"I am," I replied wearily. He stammered for a moment, then nodded and let me through the door. I walked directly through the lobby into the back of the auditorium. Detectives and uniformed officers swarmed the stage. George was speaking to a detective near the stage. And then I saw Cherry.

What I saw caused me to gasp in horror. She was tied to the chair she had sat in during the panel. Her striking white uniform was drenched with blood. I turned my head away, aghast—in all my years of sleuthing, I had never seen anything so gruesome.

My spell was broken when George spotted me. "Nancy!" she exclaimed.

The young detective who was interviewing her stopped short and took a step toward me. He was wearing a brown suit and a fedora. "Nancy Drew?" he asked.

I nodded bleakly, still shaken by the scene on stage.

"I'm Detective Ross," he explained. "We'll need your statement. I hear you had some sort of altercation with Ms. Ames during the panel tonight."

I sank into a chair at the end of a row, absentmindedly rubbing my lower back, which often grew tight when I was tense. "It was an abstract theoretical argument. Nothing personal. I was trying to make a point."

"So you and Ms. Ames were on friendly terms?"

I looked down at my hands. They were freckled with age spots. Confronted with the passage of time, my rocky relationship with Cherry suddenly seemed a great waste. "She was my nemesis," I admitted frankly.

He looked interested. "Your nemesis? You mean enemy?"

"No. We were colleagues. We were just very different. Opposites. We played well off each other. We have a very different fan base."

"Where were you tonight?"

I told Detective Ross about our dinner out and my phone call to Ned, and how I had then fallen asleep.

He wrote something in his notebook. "Ned is your husband?"

"He used to be. Now we're just special friends."

"Special friends?"

I searched for an explanation. "We date."

"Oh."

"What happened to Cherry?"

"She was bludgeoned to death with a magnifying glass. Sometime within the last two hours. Which means sometime while you say you were asleep in your room. Do you have one?"

I reached into my purse, pulled out my heavy magnifying glass, and handed it to him.

He turned it over in his hands. "I'll have to take this down to the station."

"So I'm a suspect?"

He looked around the room and raised an eyebrow. "You all are," he replied ominously. "This is the work of a pro. As far as I'm concerned, none of you lady sleuths are leaving town until we know what happened to the nurse."

Kim Aldrich widened her blue eyes and pushed her shiny brown hair behind her ears. "They can't keep us here," she lamented, adjusting her stylish secretary's ensemble of a checkered pinafore and blouse with bow collar. "I've got to get back to WALCO, Inc. I've just taken a new secretarial course and I'm sure this time I'll get a promotion."

Kim and George and I were sipping Sanka in George's brownstone, located just off campus. We had been questioned by the police all morning, and now Judy Bolton and Donna Parker were experiencing the same treatment down at the station.

George ran a hand through her spiky gray hair and muttered, "I just can't believe that Cherry is dead. And how can they question Donna Parker? She's not quite fifteen."

"She's at least thirty," groaned Kim, "and everyone knows it. I don't know why she insists on wearing that camp outfit."

"She says she's fourteen, and we have to respect that," George cautioned. "It's her lifestyle and we can't judge it."

Kim rolled her eyes. George continued to pace around the sitting room until her lower back began to bother her and then she sat down. "Hypers!" she growled. "We've got to solve this mystery soon or the conference will be ruined!"

Kim smiled wanly. "I know shorthand. If it'll help."

George's roommate, V, brought in a fresh electric pot of coffee and refilled our mugs. V had become an artist, and the brownstone was full of her work: large watercolors of blossoming flowers. I found them quite lovely, though they made

120

me feel a little funny in a way that I couldn't identify. In any case, I considered it very admirable that George had invited V to move east with her; I had rarely seen such devoted room-mates.

The doorbell rang and Judy and Donna walked in. Once they were seated, the two women excitedly reported their experiences down at the station. They had been questioned separately for several hours, and then each girl had been required to turn over her magnifying glass, just as Kim and I had.

"They're looking for the murder weapon," I theorized. "But it's a red herring!"

"So what do we do?" quizzed Donna. The dark-haired, rose-cheeked woman looked stricken. She slumped forward and set her chin on two fists. "Oh, pooh!" she added. "I thought this was going to be fun like camp." With her headband, camp shirt, and shorts, Donna did look younger than thirty but also vaguely creepy. I had felt a nagging responsibility for the young woman since I had met her at the conference launch cocktail party. She had been inspired to teen sleuthdom after reading Carolyn's stories of my exploits, but after peaking in her middle teens, she had been unable to find success since. Trapped by the public's inability to let her age, she toured malls selling books dressed like a teenager. But she seemed to have taken her ruse a little too much to heart.

Judy sighed deeply and rose from her seat. I had always found her single-minded and politically progressive. "I think we should consider the social ramifications of inequality. Clearly there is a social problem at the heart of this matter.

121

If we can address the big picture, perhaps we can effect real change."

We all looked at her blankly.

She sat back down. "Or we can call my husband, Peter. He's in the FBI."

"Or my dad," piped in Kim. "He's in the FBI too."

"I don't think we need to call the FBI yet," I declared. "Not until we know more about what's going on."

"Golly, how do we do that?" asked Donna.

"We go back to the scene of the crime," I declared matter-of-factly. "George, do you have a key to Grover Hall?"

George grinned. "You bet I do!"

We waited until dark and then made our way to Grover Hall, where George let us in the back faculty entrance. George turned on the lights, and we all crept along the wall to the stage, so as not to destroy evidence.

"Everyone split up and look for clues," I instructed.

We climbed on stage and fanned out. Of course we were at somewhat of a disadvantage without our magnifying glasses, but several of us had reading glasses, which worked in a pinch. With so many sleuths, it didn't take long to turn up a clue.

"Goodness, look at this!" Donna exclaimed. She was standing at the side of the stage, next to where the curtain stood open. She reached into one of the folds at the base of the curtain and pulled out something small and shiny. "What is it?" she asked.

We all gathered around and examined the piece of jewelry.

"It's a sorority pin," Judy explained to Donna.

Donna looked misty eyed. "I hope one day I'm old enough to go to college."

There was an awkward silence.

Then Judy held the pin toward George. "Do you recognize it?" Judy asked.

George furrowed her thick unplucked brow. "Why, that looks like a Seven Sisters pin!" she exclaimed. She lowered her voice. "That's a secret society of female students at the seven sister colleges. It's very elite. Very hush-hush. Rumor has it that most of the women go on to join the CIA."

"It's pretty," sighed Kim.

"This pin could have been left here anytime," Judy pointed out.

George shook her head emphatically. "The curtains were taken down and cleaned right before the conference."

"So a sister must have had something to do with what happened to Cherry," I theorized. "Do they have a meeting place here on campus?"

George nodded. "There's a secret hall just up the street. They meet secretly every Saturday night at the secret hour of midnight."

"Why, that's in only one hour!" observed Donna.

Deciding that our best course of action was to go undercover, I disguised myself as a co-ed, donning blue jeans and parting my hair down the middle in the style of the day. Then I affixed the Seven Sisters pin to my college sweatshirt and went to the secret meeting hall. The others agreed to wait hidden behind trees outside until I emerged or one hour had passed.

I watched as several young women rang the doorbell and were ushered inside. With a few deep breaths to steady my nerves, I approached the large oak door, rang the bell, and waited. In a few minutes, a young woman wearing a red cloak that obscured her face opened the door.

"Uh, are you somebody's grandmother?" she asked.

"Returning student," I answered nonchalantly, drawing her attention to my pin.

She hesitated, but after glancing at the pin allowed me to enter.

Once inside the stately stone building, I watched as the women ahead of me approached a wardrobe stand hung with red cloaks just inside the door. Each donned a cloak over her clothes, poured a cup of punch, and headed downstairs to the basement.

I followed suit.

There were scores of red-clad sisters gathered in the basement of the hall, but my attention was immediately drawn to the small stage at the front of the room where an altar stood. On it was a nurse's cap!

My mind reeled. Could these women have killed Cherry? And if so, why?

A red-cloaked figure emerged from the crowd and took a position behind a podium next to the altar. She raised her arms, and all the women immediately gave her rapt attention. I was not prepared for what happened next. The figure threw back her hood, revealing straight hair, glasses, and a serious expression. I stifled a gasp. It was the woman who had asked me a question at our panel: Madge Hollings!

With a wicked gleam in her eye, Madge Hollings walked over to the altar, picked up Cherry's cap, and placed it on her own head. Then she faced the gathered sisters.

"Sisters!" she announced. "We have an intruder amongst us! Throw back your hoods!"

They were on to me! I was trapped!

One by one the women threw back their hoods, revealing their faces. I had no choice but to do the same. Madge Holling stepped offstage and walked among us, inspecting each face. When she came to me, she stopped short.

"Nancy Drew," she hissed between clenched teeth.

How she had seen through my disguise, I'll never know. In that moment, the crowd surged forward.

When I regained consciousness I was locked in a trunk in the secret meeting hall of the secret sorority of the Seven Sisters. The coffinlike prison was just large enough for me to lie flat. I listened for sounds of my captors but heard nothing but silence. After much effort, I managed to reach down and take off one of my sneakers. Crying out for help, I knocked on the walls with it, attempted to tap out a code, but the sound did not carry. How I longed for a pump with a good hard heel! I felt a cold chill come over me as I realized that my prison tomb was airtight. Soon I would be out of oxygen!

The minutes ticked by in the darkness, and though I tried to breathe shallowly, I could feel my head growing light as the oxygen waned, and a wave of sleepiness came over me. Resolutely, I willed myself to stay awake, knowing that if I fell asleep, I might never awake.

I thought of the twinkle in Ned's soft eyes. Frank's dark hair. Ned Junior. My hometown of River Heights. The mighty Muskoka. The photos Marty sent of my father's wizened face and omnipresent oxygen tank. I thought of whispering statues and haunted bridges, of tolling bells and hollow oaks. Perhaps Frank was right. Perhaps the world of the teen sleuth was coming to a close.

I was just slipping back into unconsciousness when the small door to my prison burst open and the concerned faces of Judy, Donna, George, and Kim appeared.

"We've found her!" George cried. "She's over here!"

Presently I was lifted from the secret room into the light of the secret meeting hall basement. The room was teaming with police, and several angry-looking, red-cloaked women sat handcuffed against the wall.

"Oh, Nancy!" Kim exclaimed. "We were worried sick!"

"It was Kim who found you," George explained. "We discovered some sister meeting minutes hidden in the altar. They were written in shorthand."

"I knew that course would come in handy," Kim declared proudly. "I can also operate a mimeograph."

Detective Ross came over and kneeled beside me. "You're a courageous lady, Nancy Drew," he exclaimed admiringly. "You broke up a sorority cult and caught Cherry's killer."

My head was beginning to clear. "So Madge Hollings did kill Cherry?"

"She's confessed to everything," Detective Ross answered.

"But why did she do it?" asked George, turning to me.

"The sorority," I told her simply. "Enrollment numbers have been down. Madge thought that it was because we weren't the right kind of role models. When I told her that Cherry was Helen Wells, she thought that by getting rid of Cherry she could take over authorship of the Cherry Ames franchise. With that kind of access to young minds, Madge

"We've found her!" George cried. "She's over here!"

could mold a whole generation of teenage girls. By updating Cherry Ames as a gum-chewing, Mustang-driving, Seven Sisters sorority girl, they thought that they could create a legion of young girls who would one day join the Seven Sisters. Of course," I added matter-of-factly, "what she didn't realize is that Cherry lost her publishing contract years ago."

"She really thought we were poor role models?" Judy asked, aghast.

"Why, that's absurd!" gulped Donna, wide-eyed. "We're all role models in our own way, within the context of our era."

"That's right," I declared meaningfully to Donna. "Our characters offer girls independent, plucky protagonists who can problem-solve and escape from pirates. But we are also role models beyond that—as real human beings. We have the opportunity to show our readers that they can grow up and go out into the world and evolve as people without abandoning the curiosity and smarts of our spirited youth."

"I couldn't have said it better myself," agreed Judy.

Donna's bottom lip started to tremble. "But sometimes I don't think they want us to grow up."

"It's their youth they want to hang on to," I told her gently. "Not ours."

She looked at me questioningly, and then her eyes narrowed with determination. We all watched as she slowly reached up and pulled off her headband. She held it in her hands for a moment, then let it drop to the floor. Relief washed over her face.

"Good girl," I declared, patting her on the hand.

"There's one thing I don't understand," mused George. "Why did Madge use a magnifying glass?"

"She could have been trying to frame us," I theorized. "But I don't think that Madge was that smart. It's more likely that it was just the weapon she had handy."

"She said that she used a magnifying glass for a biology class," Detective Ross declared. "She was studying entomology."

The girls smiled widely in appreciation of my detection abilities.

Detective Ross grinned as well and opened a large briefcase he had beside him. Inside were several magnifying glasses, tagged and placed in evidence bags. He pulled them all out and distributed them to the group. He placed the largest and heaviest magnifying glass into my hands. "I believe that this belongs to you."

IX THE HAUNTED CRUISE SHIP, 1985

"Ned, look out!" I shouted.

Startled, Ned was able to step out of the way of my speeding shuffleboard puck in the nick of time, avoiding serious injury.

We were onboard the *Atlantic Queen*, cruising from New York City to Bermuda. In his retirement, Ned had become a daytime television enthusiast. Whether this had led to his depression, or vice versa, I am still unclear. In any case, Ned had become interested in the New Age movement after seeing Shirley MacLaine interviewed on *The Phil Donahue Show*. When he found out about a New Age–themed cruise through the Bermuda Triangle, there was no dissuading him.

"You're so competitive!" Ned cried. "You know that's a past-life issue."

I put down my shuffleboard cue. "Why don't we just stroll?" I suggested.

We walked, arm in arm, along the promenade deck. I gazed up at my tall and attractive special friend. His hair had thinned and he had grown out what was left into a sort of elderly mullet. His jowls had sunk and his eyebrows had grown white and wild. He insisted on wearing a Members Only jacket. He bought a DeLorean. And now he carried crystals in his pockets to ward off dark angels. I was beginning to worry that my old friend might be having some sort of late-life crisis.

"Do you think I'm still handsome and athletic looking?" he inquired shyly as we walked.

I grinned. "You bet I do!"

"And broad shouldered and attractive?"

"Absolutely."

He squeezed my hand affectionately. We continued walking, arm in arm, in silence until Ned broke the spell.

"Are you planning on going to the UFO-spotting class at three?" he asked brightly.

"I've got Jazzercise," I told him.

I had been taking Jazzercise every day since we had boarded three days before, mostly in an effort to avoid the many seminars on transcending planes of existence and channeling the dead. Because I was well into my seventies, for insurance reasons the cruise operators made me take the class sitting down. This suited me just fine. The instructor, a young woman who wore her striped leotard, leg warmers, and fingerless lace gloves even when off-duty, was named Mandy. She was slim and short, with well-defined quads and tightly curled orange hair.

At three o'clock, Mandy led class as usual, though I noticed that she seemed somewhat sluggish and perhaps a little bloated. After class I approached her and asked her if she was feeling well.

She told me that she had not slept soundly the night before, due to a strange, insistent knocking at her cabin door. But whenever she got up to answer the knocking, the corridor was deserted.

"Probably just children playing a prank," she remarked, dabbing the sweat on her face with a hand towel.

That night, Ned and I attended a lecture on healing crystals, visited the discotheque in the Twilight Room, and then turned in. A little after two in the morning, we both awoke with a start. Someone was knocking on the door to our cabin! I listened for a moment. The knocking grew louder. Remembering Mandy's story, I hesitated to answer the door, as to do so might only encourage the prankster. But what if someone was in trouble?

Ned sat up. "What's going on?" he asked sleepily.

"That's what I'd like to know," I told him.

Gathering my wits, I put on my terry cloth robe and crept quickly toward the door, with Ned doddering behind me.

But when we opened it, the corridor was deserted! Curious, I stepped into the hallway and craned to see around the corner, just in time to catch a flash of someone scurrying out of sight! Without regard to my personal safety, I hurried after him. Ned hurried after me. When we rounded the corner, we came face to face with a doughy, middle-aged man with bad skin and large black plastic eyeglasses with very thick lenses. He was wearing a stained undershirt and striped pajamas.

"Who are you?" I demanded.

The odd-looking man stood his ground. "Who are you?" he retorted.

"Who are you?" Ned shot back.

The man drummed his dirty fingernails on the edge of his receding hairline and closed his eyes in deep thought. Then he opened them. "You're Nancy Drew," he announced with a satisfied smile. "The knocking woke you up too. And now you are both after the perpetrator."

I was flummoxed. "How did you know that?"

"Guess!"

I was taken aback. "Excuse me?"

133

"Guess! Please. I love it when people guess. Guess! Guess! Guess!"

"I don't have time for this," I told him, turning back toward my cabin. "Come on, Ned."

The man hurried awkwardly after us. "My name's Encyclopedia Brown," he answered, "and I'm a detective."

"Encyclopedia Brown," I repeated. "America's Sherlock Holmes in sneakers."

His doughy face brightened. "You've heard of me?"

"Once or twice."

"So do you want to help me solve the mystery?"

"Help you?" I asked. "I think you'd be helping me. Besides, as far as I know there is no mystery," I told Encyclopedia. "Just someone playing a prank. For all I know, that someone is you." I pointed a bony finger at him. "You were a precocious boy detective with all the promise of the world laid out before you. Now look at you: you're a middle-aged man with poor hygiene. You probably still live with your parents. I'd wager you could stand a little excitement."

His posture stiffened defensively. "What kind of loser would still live with his parents?"

The lights in the corridor suddenly went out, and we were plunged into darkness.

"W-w-what's going on?" Encyclopedia stammered in the dark.

"Shh!" I told him.

"Listen," whispered Ned.

A low moaning sound emanated from the far end of the hall. I peered in its direction and was disconcerted to see a light floating toward us. As it grew closer I could make out the image of a ghostly young girl wearing a long white dress. She wore a gold locket around her neck and was levitating several feet off the ground.

"It's an angel!" Ned mooned.

The lights came back on as suddenly as they had gone off, and she had vanished! I glanced at Encyclopedia. His pimply face was ashen. Ned gazed saucer-eyed at the place where the angel had been.

A uniformed porter came dashing toward us. "Are you old folks okay?" he asked solicitously.

"We're fine," I responded. "What happened?"

"Some sort of power failure, just on this deck," he explained. "I better go check on the other passengers." He continued past us down the hallway.

"You didn't tell him about the ghost," observed Encyclopedia when the porter was out of sight.

"That was no ghost," Ned exclaimed. "That was an angel. From Mesopotamia."

I took Encyclopedia aside. "I find that it's a good idea not to scare people with ghost stories until the ghosts are thoroughly investigated," I told him. "They are almost always people dressed in muslin trying to scare everyone off so they can locate a treasure or get a good price on a house."

Encyclopedia considered this. "You know, I've read all your books," he remarked. He puffed out his chest a little. "I've read more books than anyone else in Idaville, Florida."

"You read Nancy Drew books?" I asked, raising an eyebrow.

"Yes," he admitted bravely. He looked down at his stained undershirt and pulled awkwardly at it. "I do still live with my parents," he mumbled. "But I'm planning on moving out just as soon as I finish the computer language I'm writing."

I patted Encyclopedia on his flabby arm. "You better be getting back to your room," I told him kindly.

He nodded several times.

"Now," I told him.

"Okay. Good night." He slumped off down the corridor.

"Good night," I called. I walked back over to Ned.

"This proves it," he told me excitedly. "I had my doubts. But now I know that Shirley was right about everything."

"Let's go back to the room," I sighed.

Back in our cabin, Ned fell asleep quickly, despite his apnea. Tomorrow, I told myself, I would get to the bottom of this alleged ghost business. Someone was trying to fool us into believing a lot of hogwash. And I didn't like it one bit.

"Have you ever seen an angel before?" I asked Ned.

"What?" replied Ned, looking up from the Rubik's Cube he was worrying. We were enjoying our breakfast on deck beside all of the young people in swimsuits. I was writing a postcard to Ned Junior, Foxy, and their three boys, Jupiter, Pete, and Bob, named after some friends from California. (Foxy had taken the unfortunate name of Foxy Belden-Frayne-Nickerson, which, when written on a postcard, left little room for a message.) Suddenly, who should appear but Encyclopedia Brown with his parents in tow. He was wearing a snug Dungeons & Dragons T-shirt, Bermuda shorts, red knee socks, and loafers, and he was making a beeline right for us.

"Good morning!" Encyclopedia exclaimed too loudly.

"This is my mother, Mrs. Brown, and my father, Chief Brown." Chief Brown was wearing a police uniform.

"Is there a problem, Officer?" asked Ned cautiously.

Chief Brown laughed. "Oh, no! I'm on vacation." He cleared his throat. "I just like to wear the uniform."

"I see," commented Ned.

Encyclopedia grinned proudly. "I wanted Mom and Dad to meet my new friends." He turned to his parents. "See," he exclaimed, "I wasn't lying."

Mrs. Brown looked surprised and pleased. "Well, isn't that nice," she declared.

Encyclopedia flung himself down in the chair next to Ned, picked up his Rubik's Cube from the table, and began to turn it with lightning speed. "The folks are going to the harp concert today, so I thought I could hang out with you guys." He set the solved Rubik's Cube back in front of Ned. Ned's face fell.

"Today's not good for me," I explained frankly. "I've got Jazzercise."

"That's okay!" Encyclopedia retorted. "I can tag along. I love to dance!"

I glanced skeptically at Encyclopedia's flaccid girth.

Mrs. Brown smiled. "It's so nice to see Encyclopedia making acquaintances." She kissed him on the forehead. "We'll see you tonight, dear." She and Chief Brown were gone before Ned or I could say another word.

Encyclopedia shrugged. "I think they miss Idaville," he confided. He leaned toward me and smiled conspiratorially. "Guess what I have in my pocket!" he whispered, eyes sparkling with excitement.

I wrinkled my face. "No."

"Come on!" he insisted. "Guess."

"I don't know," I declared firmly.

He pursed him lips and pulled a brochure from the back pocket of his shorts and carefully spread it out on the table. "The activities director gave me this," he explained. The brochure had an underwater photograph of divers on it along with a story of a local shipwreck. Encyclopedia summarized. "In the early 1600s, a rich sea captain came over from England. He made his fortune and then sent for his young daughter to join him. The ship she was on went down in the Bermuda Triangle." Encyclopedia pointed gravely to a sketch of the young girl.

"Why, she's the spitting image of the ghost in the corridor!" I exclaimed.

"Hey!" exclaimed Ned. "That looks like my angel!"

"Is that shipwreck near here?" I asked Encyclopedia.

Encyclopedia nodded, grinning. "There's a diving expedition this afternoon!"

Ned put his hands on his knees and shakily stood up. "I'll sign us up for that dive!"

"Are you sure?" I asked. "I know you were looking forward to that aura encounter group at three."

"My aura can wait," Ned replied, his elderly eyes bright with purpose. "This angel is real, and I'm going to prove it."

That left us two hours to fill. Encyclopedia and I decided to change into our Jazzercise clothes and go back and interview our first witness: Mandy.

Encyclopedia Brown could dance! His moves were a little clumsy, and his perspiration copious, but he had heart and was amazingly quick on his Reeboks. Even Mandy was impressed at how well he could keep up. His net half shirt, however, was a little revealing, and I noticed that several women ducked out of class early.

"I'm a big Liza Minnelli fan," I overheard Encyclopedia tell Mandy, cleaning his sweat-fogged glasses with his thumb. "I have been for years."

"Me too!" exclaimed Mandy. "You used to be that boy genius, right? Sherlock Holmes in short pants?"

"Sneakers," Encyclopedia corrected her, his face reddening at the female attention.

Mandy was unfazed. "Whatever."

I told Mandy that Encyclopedia and I were looking into the knocking mystery.

Delighted by our interest, Mandy told us that the knocking had woken her three nights in a row and that nearly half of her students had reported similar experiences! Like Ned, several had reported seeing an angel. Word had spread, and now many of the hallways belowdecks were lined with passengers camped out in hopes of seeing the celestial vision. The corridors were thick with incense. Someone was even selling angel catcher nets. Mandy seemed quite distressed by all of this.

With all of the excitement, we were the only three passengers to show up for the shipwreck dive.

Our instructor was a blond mustachioed man in his thirties. In my ongoing effort to keep my keen eye for detail sharp, I observed that he was tanned a deep bronze and had ample chest hair. He wore a pair of black Italian bikini swim trunks, which complimented his already impressive physique.

139

As we made our way by boat to the dive site, the mustachioed man explained some more about the shipwreck. The wreck, he said, had been particularly mysterious, as the ship had gone down in fair weather and without warning in the Bermuda Triangle. Rumor was that the sea captain's daughter was traveling with the captain's treasure and that pirates may have boarded the ship and then sunk it. Until he died, the sea captain refused to believe that the girl had gone down with the ship, and he spent the last years of his life searching the surrounding islands for her, hoping that she had somehow survived.

We anchored over the wreck and strapped on our gear. Encyclopedia put his glasses away and strapped on his prescription goggles.

The ocean in that area was not deep, and we could see the wreck clearly through the blue water, just thirty feet below us. I motioned for the others to follow and began my descent in my skirted one-piece, with the instructor close on my flippers. There was not much left of the ship, only a wooden skeleton that had long ago become a home to a rich variety of marine life. I swam down to the white sand on the ocean floor and sifted through it with my hands in hopes of finding some clue that had eluded the hundreds of divers who had come before me. I saw Encyclopedia and Ned doing the same.

Time seemed to slow as we searched, listening only to the sound of our own breathing. Suddenly I felt a hand grip me firmly around the ankle! I spun around underwater, ready to confront my assailer, only to find a grinning Encyclopedia. He held out his open hand. In it was a locket identical to the one the ghost in the corridor had worn!

Suddenly I felt a hand grip me firmly around the ankle!

I felt another hand grip my ankle! This time it was Ned, his gray hair fanned out wildly in the water around his head. He motioned to his air pressure gauge. It was almost at zero, which meant that our oxygen was getting low. He thrust his thumb toward the surface and we began our slow ascent. When we broke the surface of the water and took off our masks, the dive boat was gone. It was hard to tell from the surface of the water, but it looked as if the ship was gone too! We were alone. In the middle of the Bermuda Triangle!

Encyclopedia, Ned, and I turned our heads frantically, looking for any sign of a boat or diver, and we paddled madly to keep our heads above water. The sea was getting choppy as a wind picked up. Where had our dive instructor gone? Had we been forgotten, or was this some wicked plot to leave us to our deaths?

I called to Ned and Encyclopedia to remain calm and instructed them to follow me. We had to try to swim to one of the nearby islands. I put my mask back in place and, using a butterfly stroke, I led the two boys toward a horizon of sand in the distance. Using all the skill I'd learned as a summer lifeguard, I pushed forward through the waves.

Even when my muscles began to cramp and my lungs ached, I forced myself to continue. When Ned seemed to fail, I waved Encyclopedia over to him, and Encyclopedia pulled Ned's frail arms around his plump shoulders and carried him on his back. When we finally reached the island of our salvation, the sun had set and we could just make out the island's silhouette in the waning evening light. Encyclopedia and I dragged Ned to shore and collapsed in exhaustion on the white sand.

We slept until sunrise.

When we awoke, the day was again calm. The island was a stretch of beach with a clutch of palm trees and bushes at its center. A flock of seagulls squawked noisily on the shore. I gazed out on the sparkling blue horizon of ocean and gave a small shout of delight.

Ned awoke. "What happened?" he asked, rubbing his eyes.

I stood up and pointed. "There! It's the ship! They haven't left yet!"

Encyclopedia and Ned sat up excitedly. In the distance the ship sat clear as day, a white square on a bed of blue.

Encyclopedia pulled on his prescription goggles so he could see it. "We'll need to fashion a flare or bonfire or something," he suggested.

"How?" asked Ned, looking around at the deserted island.

Encyclopedia closed his eyes and stood deep in thought, and then he turned to me. "Do you have your magnifying glass?" he asked.

I looked down at my skirted one-piece. "Only my travel one," I answered. I reached into the cup of my padded bosom and produced a small plastic magnifying glass about the size of an adult pinky. I handed it to him.

"Perfect!" he exclaimed. "I'll use a focused ray of sun to set a palm tree on fire. They're sure to spot it from the ship."

"Good thinking!" complimented Ned.

Encyclopedia took a few steps toward the center of the island, where he stopped short. "Look at this," he declared slowly.

Ned and I looked where Encyclopedia was pointing. There were footprints. And they looked fresh!

We decided to follow them.

I went first, followed by Ned, with Encyclopedia, still in his goggles, his pale hairy belly hanging over his rainbow swim trunks, bringing up the rear. We followed the footprints in the sand toward the brush at the center of the island, where they suddenly turned and headed south around the brush and back toward the beach. The prints followed the beach around to the far side of the island and back up toward the brush. A dive boat was anchored off shore, and a man was digging at the base of a palm tree. It was our blond mustachioed dive instructor! He had changed from the black bikini briefs into a Hawaiian shirt, surf shorts, and sneakers.

He looked up from his hole and raised his shovel threateningly. His face was twisted into a menacing scowl.

Encyclopedia stepped forward. "I know that you're behind the ghost in the corridor and the knocking," he declared confidently.

The mustachioed man cocked his head with interest.

"I also know what your motive is!" Encyclopedia continued.

The mustachioed man raised his shovel higher.

"And I can prove it!" Encyclopedia added emphatically.

This seemed to startle the man. He stared at the paunchy, shirtless detective with his hard green eyes. "Okay, nerd," the man growled. "What exactly do you think you know?"

Encyclopedia threw him a satisfied smiled. "Guess!"

"Encyclopedia," Ned warned slowly. The mustachioed man looked very strong, and we were two small, elderly people and one awkward-looking middle-aged man with adult acne. This concerned me.

"Come on! Guess!" Encyclopedia continued unfazed, his hands on his hips. "I'll tell you only if you guess!"

The mustachioed man hesitated, and for a moment I feared that he might rush us with his gardening tool. I braced myself for a confrontation, but to my surprise he put down the shovel, and his posture softened. "Do you think it's because of Mandy?" he asked, his voice cracking.

I tried to hide my surprise. Mandy, my Jazzercise instructor, couldn't be involved in such a dirty plot as this! Could she?

Encyclopedia nodded. "Mandy," he agreed.

"You probably think it's because Mandy wants out of her contract with the ship. Because she got that job offer to be Jane Fonda's personal trainer. You probably think this was all her idea to fake the haunting stuff so the cruise would be shut down and that she had me wrapped around her little finger."

"But it wasn't working," I broke in. "The passengers were mistaking your Super Eight projection apparition for an angel. The cruise would have been more popular than ever. You planted the locket so we would believe the ghost story. But then we took too long to find it and you panicked and left us, thinking you'd blame our deaths on the ghost and they would shut down the cruise for sure! Now you're here burying a so-called treasure that will reinforce your ghost ruse!"

"Hey," the mustachioed man whined, "*I'm* guessing."

"Sorry."

He continued. "I bet that you think that I'm burying all the evidence connecting Mandy and me to the fake ghost and Jane Fonda." He searched Encyclopedia for approval. "Am I right, nerd?"

Encyclopedia nodded. "You're right."

We escorted the mustachioed man and all the evidence back to the ship via the diving boat. We were greeted enthusiastically by the crew and passengers, who had been worrying about us most of the night after our dive instructor returned without us, telling some strange story about a ghostly apparition and then just as quickly disappearing himself. Mrs. Brown and Chief Brown were especially pleased to see their son, as they had feared the worst had happened while they had been gambling, drinking strawberry daiquiris, and generally enjoying themselves for the first time in years.

We handed our prisoner over to the captain and recounted the entire story and the mustachioed man's strange confession.

"Where's Mandy?" I demanded. "Where's Mandy the Jazzercise instructor?"

The crowd parted, revealing Mandy, who stood angrily glaring at her mustachioed accomplice.

"I had to tell them!" he cried. "The nerd knew everything!"

Mandy scowled. "Okay, you caught me," she admitted. "I was behind the whole business. All I ever wanted to do was go to Hollywood to train the stars, and when I got offered the Jane Fonda job I couldn't give it up just because of some stupid cruise ship contract."

"But what's the connection to the original shipwreck?" Ned asked, perplexed.

Encyclopedia pulled out of his mother's embrace. "There was no girl." He announced, turning to the captain. "And no shipwreck. Was there, Captain?"

The captain cleared his throat. "How did you know?" he asked, chagrined.

Encyclopedia shrugged self-effacingly. "I guessed."

"What do you mean, no shipwreck?" inquired Ned.

The captain sighed. "We made up all that stuff about the shipwreck. It's just something we put together for the tourists. All part of the package. The shipwreck is made of plastic and Styrofoam. We did the brochure with a mimeograph machine."

"So the knocking was a hoax," I declared. "The ghost-angel was a hoax. And the shipwreck itself was a hoax!"

Everyone on deck applauded my astute summary.

But I noticed Ned turn away, his eyes downcast.

I came up behind him and put my frail arms around him. "I'm sorry she didn't turn out to be an angel," I whispered.

He blushed. "I just wanted to believe in something," he explained. He looked out at the expanse of ocean and his eyes watered. "Sometimes I feel so afraid."

"Of what?" I asked kindly.

"Of getting older. I watch my shows and they just remind me how life is passing me by."

"Life isn't passing you by," I told him. "We've had so many adventures, Ned. And we'll have more."

"I don't want adventure." His eyes met mine. "I just want to spend time with you. That's all I've ever wanted."

"Really?" I squeezed his frail hands in mine. "I love you, Ned Nickerson."

"I love you, Nancy Drew."

Encyclopedia appeared beside us, grinning. "Guess what? The captain just asked me to host the ship's next cruise! They're launching a new theme: Murder at Sea. With dinner theater and everything!"

"That sounds perfect," I told him.

147

That night while Encyclopedia was breaking the news to his elated parents, Ned and I attended the Atlantic Pacific New Age Ball. We danced until dawn.

We may have had our ups and downs, but no one could ever Lindy with me like Ned could.

X THE SECRET OF CAROLYN KEENE, 1992

"Do you miss Dad?" Ned Junior asked.

"Of course," I answered.

I was at Crabapple Farm where Foxy and Ned Junior now lived in Sleepyside-on-the-Hudson, New York. Ned had died two years before. He had a massive heart attack during an impromptu game of touch football at the Emerson College sixtieth reunion. He was eighty-two. Our last years together had truly been our happiest, full of travel and romance.

I missed him most on Sunday evenings, a night we always spent together. It was a long time before I could watch *Murder, She Wrote* without him.

"I loved your father very much," I told Ned Junior, patting him on the hand. And it was true. I had loved both his fathers.

We were sitting on the porch of the wooden farmhouse overlooking the vegetable garden where Foxy was transplanting some tomato plants. The boys were teenagers now. Each knew how to treat a copperhead bite and track a bobcat. Ned Junior was almost fifty and had grown into a handsome, confident man. His titian hair was flecked with gray and laugh lines creased his face. He taught at Vassar and had spent the last several years writing a book about a single Herman Melville poem. (He said that I had taught him to look closely at things). He and Foxy were still very much in love.

"Do you ever think about Ai Sato?" Ned Junior asked suddenly.

I turned to look at him, surprised. "You're never asked about her before," I commented.

"I didn't think you wanted to talk about her."

We were silent for a long moment, watching the chickens peck in the yard. "I suppose that I accepted the fact that she had her own adventure to live. I wasn't meant to be a part of it. And she wasn't meant to be a part of mine. Besides," I added, "Hannah was there for me."

"Like Ned was there for me?"

I cleared my throat as this sank in. "You knew?"

"About Frank Hardy? I suspected. I read all the Hardy Boys books, remember?" He adjusted his square shoulders and thrust out his handsome profile. "It was hard to miss the resemblance."

"Are you angry?" I asked.

"Did Ned know?"

"I think he did. But we never discussed it."

Ned Junior watched Foxy in the garden. "He loved you very much."

"I know."

"Do you keep in touch with Frank Hardy?"

I told Ned Junior about my last encounter with Frank in the Haight-Ashbury district in 1967 and how I had realized that Ned and I belonged together in our own way.

"Why, that clinic closed up years ago, before Foxy and I moved east!" Ned Junior exclaimed.

"It's ancient history now," I declared firmly.

Foxy stood up and walked toward the house, brushing the

150

dirt off her gardening gloves. She grinned widely, her face especially freckled from a full day in the sun. "Gosh, you two look as serious as a couple of dapple gray mares," she laughed at us with a hoot.

I did not know what that meant, but I had learned years before that the best thing to do was smile and shrug. Which I did.

I slept restlessly that night, finally drifting into fitful slumber early in the morning. I had been especially tired lately. It was as if a weakness had settled in my spine. Sometimes, when I looked in the mirror, all I saw was skin and bones. I did not recognize myself.

When I awoke it was almost noon, and Foxy and Ned Junior and the boys had gone into town. The newspaper lay open on the kitchen table. I took out my magnifying glass to read it and saw that an article had been circled. There was also a note that read:

Thought you might be interested in this. Ned Junior

I scanned the story and saw immediately why Ned Junior had brought it to my attention. A big publishing house in New York City was throwing an anniversary bash, and they were pleased to announce that one of their most elusive authors would be making an appearance: Carolyn Keene.

My fingers went numb. I had been in many precarious situations and had faced great danger on numerous occasions, but never in my life had I felt such a sense of dread. I knew that the time had come to confront the woman whose life had been so tied to my own.

By the time Ned Junior and his family had returned home, I had packed my bags.

Despite his worry, Ned Junior agreed to drive me to the Sleepyside-on-the-Hudson train station. I promised him that I would be gone only a few days, long enough to speak to Carolyn and to look up a few old friends.

"Be careful," he warned me. "It's a big city."

I reminded him of the many cases I had solved, including the Bungalow Mystery and the lesser-known Mystery of the Haunted 1963 Volvo Sedan, for which I received a commendation from the American Automobile Association. This seemed to quiet him.

The truth was that I had not been to New York in twenty-five years, and when I exited Penn Station and was confronted with the smells of the city, the scream of the taxi cabs, and the depth of the architectural canyons, I was momentarily overwhelmed.

Flustered, I went directly by cab to the St. Moritz on Central Park and unpacked. I ordered room service, took a laxative, and fell asleep by six.

I spent the next day trying to quiet my nerves for the party. I felt old and small and worried that I was being foolish even attending. I had my white hair washed and set, my nails manicured, my feet massaged, and my makeup professionally applied. This made me feel better. As dusk fell in the city, I changed into my evening clothes: a green knit evening dress with matching handbag. No one bothered to match her handbag anymore.

I still had an hour before the party began so I decided to take a constitutional down to Fifty-sixth Street and Broadway, in the hopes of seeing the old TEEN HQ. Chris Cool and Bess Marvin never returned from their spring break trip to Havana on the eve of the revolution, and Bess had become something of a national treasure as a Cuban poet. I received the occasional postcard from the couple but had little idea how they were as most of the content was blacked out by the State Department censors. Geronimo Johnson, however, had risen through the TEEN ranks, and I often saw him in the background of newspaper photographs, most notably hovering behind Salvador Allende hours before his assassination.

As I approached the corner of Fifty-sixth and Broadway, I stopped in my tracks. The Luxury Motors Building was gone! It seemed to have vanished into thin air, replaced by a fast-food restaurant and a large retail outlet. I sighed deeply. It seemed that TEEN had become as antiquated as I had.

I was stooped lost in thought on the corner when a young man stumbled into me, nearly knocking me over on the street! I had very bad knees, and only through a great act of balance was I able to avoid a fall that might have been the end of me. The young man quickly recovered himself, apologized, and lurched on about his business. I checked my purse for my wallet. It was still safely in the side pocket next to my magnifying glass.

The publishing event was held in the lobby of a large and magnificent office building. I was able to slip in unnoticed, and no one asked me for an invitation. The event was well attended. Men in tuxedos and women in evening gowns milled graciously about the room, exchanging pleasantries. I saw several name tags that I recognized: Franklin W. Dixon,

Margaret Sutton, Jinny McDonnell, Marcia Martin, Julie Campbell, Kurt Vonnegut. A quartet played on a small stage, and a legion of waiters attended to the gathered masses.

I did not recognize her at first. She had aged. The plump cheeks had hollowed and she seemed smaller, her face wilted. Her once brown hair was now snow white and piled high on her head, held in place with bobby pins. She wore a yellow evening dress and stood with a cane, watching the crowd.

I went over and stood next to her. She did not notice me.

"Carolyn Keene," I stated finally.

She glanced up, her face showing nothing.

"It's me," I declared.

Still, she looked blank.

"Nancy Drew," I stated slowly.

She examined me quizzically, a spark of concern flashing behind her pale eyes. "Excuse me?"

My cheeks began to burn. "I'm Nancy Drew. We were roommates at college. You've made a career out of telling stories about me. It's me, Carolyn. It's me, Nancy."

Carolyn raised an eyebrow. "Come sit with me," she suggested. She led me to some ornate, high-backed chairs against a wall on the far side of the room. We took a seat and she patted me pleasantly on the leg. "A long time ago, a gentleman named Edward Stratemeyer had the idea of writing heroic children series fiction. He came up with the Hardy Boys, Tom Swift, the Bobbsey Twins, and others. Have you heard of the Bobbsey Twins?"

"I knew Flossie pretty well."

"Well, when Mr. Stratemeyer decided to feature a girl detective, he wrote an outline and sent it to me and asked if I could write it. I said yes. I was part of his writer syndicate. We all took a shot at writing the books that Mr. Stratemeyer outlined. So you see, there never was a real Nancy Drew."

"So you're saying that my friends and I are just figments of your imagination?"

"I'm saying that Nancy Drew was a figment of Mr. Stratemeyer's imagination. Though I suppose that the character eventually took on a life of her own."

"Look," I retorted, "my name is Nancy Drew. My father's name was Carson Drew. I live in River Heights. My teenage sweetheart's name was Ned Nickerson. What do you call that?"

She smiled sweetly. "Coincidence?"

"I don't know what you're trying to pull," I declared. "I just wanted to come here and make amends. I've been thinking of writing my memoir and I plan on publishing it. I thought you'd want to know. But I guess you're not ready to admit what you've done."

Carolyn looked at me with what I could only read as pity. "I guess not, dear. Can I sign a book for you, though?"

I reached into my purse and pulled out a copy of *The Hidden Staircase* and placed it on Carolyn's lap. "Here," I declared. "It's for you. There's an inscription." I turned and walked away as Carolyn cautiously opened the book. Inside I had written:

For Carolyn,
Who made my whole life different. <u>Thank you</u>.
XO,
Nancy Drew

More determined than ever to write my memoirs, I sent word to Foxy and Ned Junior that I would not be returning to Crabapple Farm and instead returned to River Heights to begin work on this manuscript.

I spent the rest of that summer at home in River Heights typing out my recollections on an electric typewriter—I had little use for computers, which seemed to me to take much of the fun out of sleuthing. It would have gone faster, but my hands were arthritic. It was early fall when I finally got to describing my last trip to New York. I had just finished recounting my literal run-in with the gentleman at the corner of Fifty-sixth and Broadway when I had a sudden hunch. I stood up and walked upstairs to my large walk-in closet where I kept my matching shoes and handbags. I had not worn the green knit evening dress since that night in New York and therefore had not carried the matching handbag either. I unpacked the handbag from its box and examined it carefully. I reached into a little-used pocket, and my gnarled fingers came across a small scrap of paper. I pulled it out. It read:

7000 Calle Noche, Mexico City. If you are looking for a mystery.

My cloudy blue eyes were fairly frolicking with enthusiasm as I clutched the note in my bent hand. Of course! The young man had not taken anything from my purse—he had put something in it! Why had it taken me so long to figure it out?

I worked frantically that week to finish the manuscript and put my things in order, for this was a mystery from which I was not sure I would be returning. I packed up the house and rented it to two pretty blond twins who had just moved out from Sweet Valley, California. Then I sent a long letter to Foxy and Ned Junior with as much explanation as I thought prudent.

Once this was all accomplished, I went straight from the post office to the River Heights Airport, where I caught the next flight to Mexico City.

I slept almost the entire way to Mexico. When we arrived, I collected my trunk at the airport baggage claim and showed a cab driver the address on the note.

His face scrunched up in concern. "*Señora*, this is a very poor part of town," he declared gravely.

I shook my white hair defiantly. "This is where I must go."

He nodded and loaded my trunk into the back of his cab.

Once we were in the car, I began to quiz him. "Are there any mysteries that you know of here in town? Missing jewels? Kidnapped princesses? Cults? That sort of thing?"

The cab driver raised his eyebrows. "All the time."

I smiled happily.

After a long drive through the winding streets above the city, we came to a stop at a stucco row house. The paint was peeling and there were bars on the windows.

"This is it," the cab driver told me. "7000 Calle Noche."

I climbed carefully out of the car, and the driver unloaded my trunk onto the sidewalk.

"Do you want me to wait until you are inside?" he asked.

"No, thank you," I retorted, handing him the fare and tip.

He glanced doubtfully between me and the house and then, with a low shake of his head, got back behind the wheel and drove off.

I took a deep breath and steadied myself before knocking on the old wooden door.

It opened almost instantly.

There stood Frank Hardy, white haired and craggy, and as handsome as the first time I met him. I felt as if my heart might burst.

"Nancy," he greeted me. "It's good to see you looking as slim and attractive as always."

I blushed.

He opened the door wide, and I walked into the house. He closed the door and followed me inside.

"I knew you'd come," he told me. "That's why I had my associate plant the address in your purse. I couldn't contact you directly. It was too dangerous."

I turned and faced him. His brown eyes sparkled. "You need my help," I declared happily. "You've come out of retirement."

"Yes," he responded, his face turning serious. "It's big, Nancy, really big. The biggest adventure yet. All the old teen sleuths are being called up. Tom Swift is waiting in the Sky Queen to take us abroad."

His eyes shone as he reached around my waist and pulled me close. "Can I count on you?" he asked.

My knees went weak. And it wasn't from arthritis. "There's something I have to mail first," I told him, thinking of the manuscript in my bag. "And then I'll have to set my hair."

He pulled me closer. "Anything you want."

Of course I would help him. Little did I know that I was about to embark on the most puzzling mystery I had solved to

His eyes shone as he reached around
my waist and pulled me close.

date, one that would challenge every skill I had nurtured since I was a preteen. For now all I knew is that it felt good to be a sleuth again. And Tom Swift could wait for a little while. Frank and I had some catching up to do.

They didn't call him Hardy for nothing.

ACKNOWLEDGMENTS

The editor wishes to thank her husband, Marc Mohan, for his keen editing eye, love, patience and, most important, for access to his extensive Hardy Boys collection. Thanks also to Diana Abu-Jaber, the first to encourage the idea; Karen Karbo, for getting the project in front of Bloomsbury; Cynthia Whitcomb, for the Nazis; and Whitney Otto, for connecting me to the fabulous Joy Harris Agency. On that note, thank you to everyone at the Joy Harris Agency and to Amanda Katz, my smart editor at Bloomsbury. Thanks to my elementary school librarian, for the steady diet of Nancy Drew books, and to Mrs. Burr for pretending not to notice when I read the books in class. I owe a great debt to Lia Miternique for the brilliant cover and interior illustrations. Lia, you are a genius designer and a fine chum to boot. Finally, thanks to my mom, Mary Cain, who always said that I should be a stand-up comedian. Or a potter. Or, barring that, a writer.

A NOTE ON THE AUTHOR

Chelsea Cain is a longtime Nancy Drew enthusiast
and the author of *The Hippie Handbook* and the
memoir *Dharma Girl*. She edited the anthology *Wild
Child*, about daughters of the counterculture. She has
written for a wide variety of publications and is
currently a humor columnist for the *Oregonian*. She
lives with her husband in Portland, Oregon.

A NOTE ON THE TYPE

The text of this book is set in Bembo. This type
was first used in 1495 by the Venetian printer Aldus
Manutius for Cardinal Bembo's *De Aetna*, and was cut
for Manutius by Francesco Griffo. It was one of the
types used by Claude Garamond (1480–1561) as a
model for his Romain de L'Université, and so it was
the forerunner of what became standard European
type for the following two centuries. Its modern form
follows the original types and was designed for
Monotype in 1929.